WayBack
Short Stories for the Soul

L. Trott-Spivey

These short stories are based on actual events and reflect the author's present recollections of experiences. Some names and characteristics have been changed, some events have been compressed and some dialogue has been recreated.

ISBN-10: 069292051X
ISBN-13: 978-0692920510

DEDICATION

To my mother

CONTENTS

ACKNOWLEDGMENTS

To my mother Lue for putting up with my stubbornness raising me as best you could. For showing me everything I need to know in order to become a great woman. I love you!

To my daddy/father Donald for teaching me to reach for my goals. For stepping in and taking care of me in spite of it all. I love you!

To my babies Emmy, Reo, Rai & Meize, for being my support team, my confidants, my heart and loves. I love you!

To Shayne for being the most beautiful, amazing and smart grandson in the world. I love you!

To Spiv for being one of the most important persons in my life. For being as patient and understanding of me as you possibly could. For meaning so much to me. I love you always!

To my sister Tori for being there when I need you especially on those roads. Rain or shine, you are always there. Thank you. I love you!

To my brothers Larry and Duron for being strong against all obstacles. We are one and we can achieve anything. I love you!

To my dad Larry for being the reason I am here today. I love you!

To Pepa for being the best grandfather in the world. For stepping in, taking care of me and making me feel so special. I love you so much!

To Grandma Burgess for being so sweet and gentle to me. For loving me and giving me such great memories with you. I love you!

To the wonderful memories of Mema. You are greatly missed.

To Ms. Quie, where do I begin…you are so wonderful to me. You have been my ear, my voice and have done things that no one would do for my family. Thank you for being the strong and positive woman you are. Thank you for meaning so much to me. I love you!

Special Thanks

To my family and friends I thank each one of you for your love and support.

Thank you to my editors Patrice and Rebecca Walker.

Thank you to my extended support team Samuel L. Walker, Calvin Goodloe, Redell Blackwell, Darryl Smith, Freddie Gavin, and Freddy Higgs.

Thank you to P. 'Kwon' Kendrick for being who you are to me. 나는 너를 사랑해. 내 친구.

Thank you to my photographer Jason Dixon.

Thank you to my Graphics Designers Jason Dixon & Sherrie Rowe.

1 ROAD TRIP

Danny and I were playing on the playground when Mama started yelling out of the window.

"Diane? Danny?" she yelled.

"Ma'am?" we answered in unison as we looked up at the tall brick building where our apartment was.

"Y'all better get up here so we can hit the highway."

"What does hit the highway mean?" Danny asked.

I shrugged my shoulders because I did not know what it meant either.

"Yes ma'am," we again answered in unison.

We started racing toward the building and fought with each other to get in the front door first. The smell of cinderblocks and faint urine lingered in the air as soon as we passed the door.

Danny made it to the elevator first but it wasn't there. I began to push the up button over and over as we both stood dancing as if it would make the elevator come down faster. Danny pushed me into the closed elevator door and the took off running up the stairs to beat me.

"You're not going to beat me, Danny, it is already here." I said as I could hear the elevator slowing down.

I ran on the elevator when the door opened and started to push the 4th floor button multiple times so it would hurry up and I could beat him. The door closed and up it went.

"No, no, no!" I said as the elevator started to slow down on the second floor. Once it stopped and the doors opened enough for me to slide through, I rushed off so I could get to the stairs to try to beat Danny.

"Diane, where you going?" our neighbor Ms. Linda asked as I whisked past her.

"I got to beat Danny, Ms. Linda," I said, barely able to talk as I ran.

As I reached the fourth floor, I realized Danny beat me because he was nowhere to be seen and my mama was standing in the door with her hands on her hips and a wet dishcloth hanging from one of her hands.

"Get your tail in here," she said.

"Uh oh," I thought, because I already knew the dish cloth was to whack me on the bottom as I tried to go past her.

I immediately began to mentally calculate how fast I could get past her to make her miss hitting me. The closer I got to her, the slower I walked and the more I calculated. I could see Danny sticking his fingers in his ear wiggling his hands at me and sticking his tongue out at me laughing behind Mama.

"Danny," she said, turning towards him.

As soon as she turned, I took the opportunity to dart past her.

"Di…!" she said as she swung the dish cloth.

"Ouch!" I yelled as the wet cloth stung me through my play shorts.

"Didn't I tell y'all not to get dirty?" she asked, hitting me two more times.

I could hear Danny laughing at me.

"Yes, ma'am," I said.

As I answered I heard the dish cloth but didn't feel the hit.

"Stop picking," Mama said, whacking Danny on the arm with the dishcloth.

I looked at Danny as he looked at me with tears in his eyes. I stuck my tongue out at him and smiled at him for getting hit too.

"Diane, go in the bathroom and take a quick bath. Don't let that water out so Danny can take a quick one and we can leave," Mama said.

"Yes, ma'am," I said, going towards the bathroom.

Danny ran past me towards our room and yanked one of my ponytails.

"Ouch!" I yelled.

"Y'all gonna make me beat y'all butt, you hear me?" Mama said.

"Yes, ma'am," we said as Danny peeked out of the room door.

"That's why I'm gonna pee in the water," I told Danny, rolling my eyes and head as I slammed the bathroom door.

"Ew!" Danny said as he closed our room door.

Mama had covers, pillows and suitcases sitting at the door and told us to grab one of the suitcases and help her get them to the trunk of the car. Danny got the lightest one, of course.

"Mama, where are we going?" I asked as we were getting on the elevator.

"We are going down south," she said.

"Are we going to be in the car for a long time?" Danny asked.

"Well, it may seem like a long time to you, but it's not that long," she said.

We got off the elevator and walked to the car, sitting the suitcases at the back of the car.

"Here, take this and put it up front," Mama said, handing me a plastic grocery store bag.

As I walked the bag to the front, I could smell what smelled like some type of fried meat coming out of the bag. When I put the bag in the seat, I looked back at her and Danny and saw that she was trying to get everything in the trunk organized so I started touching the wrapped up food in the bag. I opened one of the aluminum foils and saw fried chicken legs wrapped in paper towel. I quickly closed it up, then I opened another aluminum foil which had sandwiches in them.

"No candy?" I thought as I felt a smack to the back of my head.

"Get out of there," Mama said.

"Yes, ma'am," I said, shocked by being caught inside of the bag. "Mama, you left the trunk open," I said.

"Oh, lord," she said.

"I'll close it Mama," I said.

"No, baby, it's too tall and I don't want you to get your fingers caught."

I walked past the trunk and even though it had all our bags in it, it was so big I could still lay down and have room.

As I got to the passenger side of the car, Danny was sitting in the seat.

"Move Danny, the oldest sits up front," I said.

"No, I was here first," he said.

I started pulling his arm and he started yelling.

"Stop it, Diane! I was here first! Stop it!" he said.

"Y'all both stop it!" Mama said. "Now both of y'all get in the back seat!"

"Aw, man, that's not fair," Danny said.

We both got in the back seat. Danny sat all the way on one side and I sat all the way on the other side so we wouldn't touch each other.

Mama started the car and turned on the gospel station and we started to leave. I looked out the window and waived at my friends who were still playing.

"Mama, are we going to somebody's house?" Danny asked.

"Yes, we are going to see our other family," she said.

"We have more family? I asked.

"Oh yes, we have lots and lots of family," she said.

We didn't drive long and Mama stopped.

"We here already?" Danny asked.

"No, now get out," Mama said.

We were at a corner store. We started to race in and Mama started yelling.

"Hold it! Don't you take another step," she said. "Now, we are about to go in this store and you will not act like a bunch of heathens. You will hold hands and not touch nothing, do you hear me?"

"Yes, ma'am," we said.

"I will ask you what you want and you tell me yes or no but you better not touch anything in this store."

"Yes ma'am."

We went in the store and Mama got a hand basket. She put some sodas, potato chips, and cookies in the basket. She went to a cooler and pulled out a bag of ice.

"Diane, let go of your brother's hand and hold this ice," she said.

I let go of him and held the ice. It was so cold that I wanted to hold it by the plastic at the top, but I couldn't hold it with one hand because it was too heavy for me.

She walked over to the Styrofoam coolers and handed it to Danny. We went to the little toy section and Mama started asking what we wanted.

"Ooh, Mama, can I have a pack of Garbage Pail Kids Cards?"

"Ok, is that it?" she asked.

"Can I get the Colorform?" I asked.

"Ok, but don't have all those pieces in my car," she said. "What about you, Danny?"

"Um, GI Joe and ThunderCats." he said.

"Ok," she said, putting it in her basket.

Danny and I started picking up toys, fussing at each other about which toy was the best and all of a sudden, we noticed Mama had not moved. When we looked up, she had her eyes squinted real low with a look of utter anger.

We knew this was the look of "I'm going to skin y'all butts alive." We dropped the toys and grabbed each other's hands.

We walked to the counter so we could pay.

"Hi, Sheila," the cashier said.

"Hi, Rob, how are you?"

"I am doing great. How are you guys doing?" he asked me and Danny.

"Fine," we said as I sat the ice down.

"Rob, I know there is not public bathroom here, but can they use the bathroom? We are headed down south and I forgot to make sure they went before we left."

"Sure," he said. "Come on." He lifted up what looked like a piece of wood to let us behind the counter. "I'll be right back, Sheila." he said, walking us between cans and boxes of food to an old dirty bathroom.

"Ok, you guys be careful and make sure you wash your hands," he said. "Do you remember your way back?" he asked.

"I do," Danny said.

"OK, well see you in a few," he said, walking off.

I let Danny go first since I was the oldest and could protect him.

"Danny, do not sit on the toilet, do you want me to put tissue on it?" I said.

"No, Diane! I don't have to doo-doo I have to pee- pee," he said.

"OK, well don't touch nothing," I said.

"OK," he said, going in.

I waited until he finished, which did not take too long, and started to go in.

"Stay right here. Don't move, ok?" I told him.

"OK," he said.

I went in the bathroom and started putting the tissue on the seat. Mama taught me to not touch the toilet handle, sink handle or door knob, to only use tissue. So I made sure I did exactly that. After I washed my hands I went to dry them and realized the sink drying towel was too tall for Danny. I opened the door with the tissue.

"Danny, did you wash your hands?

"No," Danny said nervously.

"Come here, I will help you."

Mr. Rob came back to the bathroom.

"Are y'all ok?" he said from outside the bathroom.

"Yes, sir," I said as if I were losing my breath.

"I'm going to open the door," he said.

"OK."

Mr. Rob walked in to see me holding Danny up as high as I could so he could reach the drying towel.

"Oh no, I will get you a napkin. The towel only spins around in there so you can use it but it won't reach down far enough for him. I don't want you to hurt yourself. Go ahead and put him down."

"So other people dry their hands on the same towel?" I asked.

"That's right," Mr. Rob said.

"Ew," Danny said.

Mr. Rob laughed. He walked us back up to where Mama was, but she wasn't there anymore.

"She is putting everything in the car," he said, handing Danny a towel. "Go ahead to her and you all have a safe trip."

"Bye!" we said, running out of the store and racing to the front seat.

"Back?" we heard Mama say, standing outside the car.

"Yes, ma'am."

We got in the car and she had already had out toys in the back seat.

"Y'all ready?" she asked.

"Yes," we said with excitement.

"OK, 95 South here we come."

"What's 95 South?" Danny asked.

"Probably a lottery number," I answered.

We rode in the car for what seemed to us to be a long time, playing with our toys.

"Going down south is boring," I told Danny.

"What's boring?" Danny asked.

"Never mind," I said.

"Mama, I'm hungry," Danny said.

"Me too," I said.

"OK. I have to get some gas, so I will stop at the next exit."

"Where are we Mama?" I asked.

"I don't know, we on the highway somewhere,"

she said.

I looked out the window to see the big blue sign with different pictures on it. The two that stuck out to me was McDonald's and the 76 gas station.

"We are going to McDonald's, Danny," I said.

"Yay!" he said.

We pulled in the gas station and Mama got out. "Do y'all have to go to the bathroom?"

"No, ma'am," we answered.

"Stay here. I'm going to get some gas and get y'all something to eat."

We stayed in the car and started playing with our toys.

"I'm going to get a Happy Meal," Danny said.

"Me too," I said.

"They got Playmobil in the Happy Meals, too," he said.

"Wow," I said.

Although we were excited about going to McDonald's, we were getting very tired. We could hear Mama in the trunk and pumping gas.

Danny got on his knees to look outside.

"Diane, I don't see any buildings. It looks different," he said.

"Different?" I asked, looking out of my window. "Whoa. What kind of gas station is this?"

"I don't know," Danny said.

We heard the trunk slam and turned around like we hadn't gotten up.

"Here," Mama said, handing us aluminum foil, a bag of potato chips, a box of cookies, and juice.

"Eat that, and I know that you will have to go to the bathroom soon, but we are going to hit the road some more."

"I thought we were going to McDonalds," Danny said.

"That is your McDonald's," Mama said.

We looked at each other, sad because we really wanted McDonald's, but we went ahead and ate our sandwich, chips, and cookies and drank our juice.

I could tell Danny was becoming antsy. He was wiggling and moving around.

"Danny, what's wrong?" I asked and he

quickly put his hands behind his back.

"Nothing," he said.

"What are you doing?" I asked.

"Nothing," he replied.

I wrestled him until Mama broke up the wrestling and said, "Hand me my Floaters 8-track."

Just as she was asking, I could see the tape strip Danny was pulling out of none other than the Floaters 8-track.

"Oooo," I said. "You're in trouble."

Just as Danny was starting to cry Mama found a station.

"Oh, here's a station," she said.

Danny, still antsy, reached in his pocket and pulled out a Zagnut bar, wax bottles, orange juice bubble gum, and a pack of King candy cigarettes.

"Where did you get that?" I asked.

"Shhhh," Danny said.

"Oooooo," I said. "You stole that out of that store."

"Don't tell on me and I will give you half,"

Danny said.

"No, I'm telling and you are going to jail and then I will have the room to myself."

"No, please," Danny begged, starting to cry.

"What's going on back there?" Mama asked as she was trying to tune the station she found.

"Nothing," Danny said."

"Y'all stop all that fighting," Mama said.

"Throw it away and I won't tell," I said.

"OK," he said and tried to roll down the window.

He wasn't strong enough for the knob, so I leaned over and helped him roll it down. He looked at me as if he wanted me to tell him to keep it. I grabbed the Zagnut bar and threw it out the window.

"Hurry up," I said.

"Roll that window up," Mama said.

"Yes, ma'am," I said.

Danny threw out the rest of the candy and folded his arms, pouting, as I rolled the window back up.

"If you steal again, I'm telling mama."

"I won't."

"You promise?" I asked.

"I promise," he said.

"Well, pinky promise, then," I said.

He wrapped his little pinky around mine in agreeance.

We started riding and I wanted to see where we were going, so I watched out of the window. I looked at the cars as they passed and the big trucks. We could hear the horns blow.

"The trucks are so big, Mama," Danny said on his knees, looking out the window.

"Yes, they are. You want to see a trick?"

"Yes, ma'am," we said.

"OK. Let me know when y'all see another truck. They are called 18-wheelers."

"Yes, ma'am"

"I see one!" I said.

"OK, I'm going to get him to blow his horn," Mama said.

"How?" Danny asked.

"Watch," she said.

The truck was approaching the car fast and she started doing a pulling motion with her arm. All of a sudden...the truck driver blew his horn.

"Wow!" we said, screaming and laughing. "Mama, how did you do that?" we asked with excitement.

"You can do it, too. When you see one, try it," she said.

We both looked out the door, eager to see a truck. It seemed like no truck was in sight. It started to get dark and we still looked outside for a truck.

"Do y'all want to play the alphabet game?" Mama said.

"Yes," we said.

"OK. We will name everything we see in the order of the alphabet, so I will start with A. Whoever sees a B first will then go, until we get to Z."

"But I don't know my alphabet good," Danny said.

"I'll help you," I said.

"Anchor!" Mama yelled.

"Anchor?" we asked.

"Yes, the lady on the board back there was a news anchor, so that's the letter A."

"Ohhh," we said.

"Now we are on B, Danny," I said.

"I gotta pee," Danny said.

"OK," Mama said. "I'll pull over in just a few minutes."

"I gotta go bad, mama," he said.

Mama pulled over to the side of the road and got out. She walked around to our side of the car and opened the door.

"Get out, Diane and Danny," Mama said. "Do you have to go too?" she asked me.

"No, ma'am," I said

"Use the bathroom right here, Danny," she said.

Having us face away from him, we stood on one side to block traffic from seeing what he was doing and the door blocked the other side.

As he finished he got in the car and Mama handed him a piece of tissue.

"Wipe your hands," she said as we drove off.

Danny looked out the window and yelled, "Blue!" continuing the game.

"Good job!" me and mama said as he smiled.

"I see one, I see one," I yelled. Danny rushed over to my side of the car and we started pulling our arm down just like Mama. We kept doing it and all of a sudden, he blew his horn. We were so happy.

"I have another trick with the 18-wheeler," she said. "I can make him cut his lights off and on."

"Really?" I asked.

"Yep, watch," she said.

Danny and I watched the truck with all its lights outside of it. There were orange lights around the bottom and top of the truck. The truck got in front of us and then it happened. He cut his lights off and on.

"Wow!" we said in amazement. "Mama, how

did you do that?" we asked.

"Mama, can we get him to do that?" Danny asked.

"No, baby, only I can. I blinked my lights to let him get in front of me because I saw his blinker on and that was him saying thank you.

"Wow, Mama, you are amazing," Danny said.

"That's my car," Danny said.

"Your car?" I asked.

"Yes, and that one too," he said, looking out of the window.

"Well, that's my car," I said.

"Nuhuh, it's mine too," Danny said, laughing.

"Limo! That's somebody famous," I said.

"Who?" Danny said.

"Anybody I want it to be," I said.

"Is it Michael Jackson?" Danny asked.

"Yep, its Michael Jackson," I said.

"Yay! I saw Michael Jackson," Danny said.

"Going down south is not boring, Danny, it's

fun," I said.

"Yep," Danny said. "Diane?" he said.

"Yes."

"I gotta pee."

"Uh oh."

Danny and I woke up to hearing Mama ordering breakfast at McDonald's.

"Mama, are we almost there?" I asked, a little tired of being in the car.

"Yes, baby, almost," she said as she took the food out of the cashier's hands.

I looked over to see Danny still asleep and we had covers and a pillow. I didn't remember Mama giving us the cover or the pillow. Come to think of it, I did not remember even making it to the window to get the McDonald's breakfast.

We were no longer on the highway; we were on what seemed to be wooded back roads. I noticed the car slowing down to stop.

"Mama, what's wrong?" I asked.

"It's a funeral," she said.

"A funeral?" I asked. "They make you stop?"

"No, baby, they don't make you stop, but out of respect of the dead, you pull over until the last car passes," she said.

"How do you know it's the last car?"

"Well, they all will have their lights on and sometimes if they have police escort, they will be at the back too."

"Oh, that's cool," I said, not realizing that the death of someone wasn't so cool.

I was sleeping comfortably until Danny started shaking me.

"Diane, Diane!" he said, sounding scared. "I think we are lost."

"Huh?" I said, waking up. The car felt like we were driving on rocks.

"Mama, are we lost? What's wrong with the

road?"

"Oh, we are on a dirt road."

"A dirt road?" we said.

"What's a dirt road?" Danny asked.

"I guess it's a road made of dirt," I answered.

"Can we fall in the dirt?" I asked as Danny got on his knees to look out the window.

"No, baby, we can't fall in," Mama said.

"We are lost, Diane," Danny said. "Look, it is only trees. There are no stores and the buildings are gone."

"Mama, are you sure we are not lost?" I asked.

"No, we are not lost."

"We lost," I said, looking at Danny.

Mama started turning. "Oh Lord!" she said and the car started tilting.

We started screaming.

"Y'all OK?" she asked.

"What's happening?" Danny asked as I slid to his side of the car.

"We in a ditch."

"What's a ditch?" Danny asked.

"Well, it's when the road is lower, or it's a deeper...Danny, I don't know I just know we in one."

"Are we going to die in the ditch?" I asked.

Mama laughed.

"No, we not gonna die in the ditch. We can just walk the rest of the way. Someone will come and get the car. It's not that far."

"Can we go to the payphone?" I asked.

"Baby, they don't have payphones out here. We can walk. It's fine," she said, opening her door, which seemed very heavy.

She helped us out of the car and we were in shock to see as far as we could in both directions nothing but woods and sand.

"Mama, I'm scared." Danny said.

"Me too," I said. "I don't like it here."

"I want to go home," Danny said, crying.

"Y'all hush up now. We will be just fine. You

will see when you get to all your cousins, you will have fun."

We started walking, and I would not let go of Danny's hand.

"You stay with me, Danny. I will protect you, OK?" I said.

"OK," he said, still crying.

"Ouch," Danny said, slapping at his arm. "Something bit me, Mama," he said.

"Oh, that's just a fly or mosquito. You will be OK. Just keep an eye out for snakes," she said, walking as if nothing was wrong.

"SNAKES?" we yelled.

"Yeah, snakes," she said, laughing.

Danny got as close to me as he could and I held Danny's hand even tighter. We walked a long time down the road. It was very hot. Bugs were flying around and Danny was still crying. We could hear in the distance what sounded like rocks.

"Oh, somebody coming. This is probably some of our kin."

"Mama, what's kin?" Danny asked.

"Oh, baby, that's what they say down here meaning one of our family members."

"So do they talk different down here?" I asked.

"Yes, a little, they will say words we don't use back home, like kin, folk, yonder, tote and other words. You will hear me say them here because that's just how we talk. They will think you are proper, but it's ok. We will all understand each other. It's still English."

"OK," I said as the sounds got closer.

"That's Richard!" Mama shouted. "He being foolish with the kids again," she said as a truck pulled up with kids sitting in the back with their feet hanging off the truck.

"Hey, Sheila!" the man said, getting out to hug Mama.

"Hi, Aunt Sheila!" the kids started saying.

"Hi, Diane! Hi Danny!" they said to us.

"They know us?" Danny asked.

"I guess so," I said.

"Hey boy, what you doing out here?" Mama said.

"Taking the kids for a ride here. When did you get here?"

"We just got here the car back there in the ditch," Mama said.

"Well shoot, that ain't no problem. Hop on in. Me and Clay will come back and get the car."

"Y'all come on. Jump in," the kids said to us.

"OK," I said, still holding on to Danny. We jumped in the back and they started hugging us. They were all excited to see us but we did not remember them.

"I'm your cousin Tasha, this is William, Brandon, Gary, and Tiffany. We are going to have fun," they said, ignoring the flies that kept landing on them. "Y'all want some candy," they said, offering their candy.

"Yes," Danny said, reaching for the candy.

"No," I said, afraid flies had been on it.

"Come on get up here," Tasha said, wanting us to climb on the back of the truck with them.

Danny jumped on the truck faster than I could blink.

"Come on, Diane," he said.

I was hesitant but climbed on the back of the truck.

When we started riding, I looked at the dirt and rocks beneath my feet and, as scared as I was, started to become excited about the ride.

"This is fun!" Danny said.

"Yeah," I said, beginning to relax.

At that time, the darkness, the woods and not even the snakes even crossed my mind. I was enjoying the night air and the ride.

We turned down another dirt road and drove to a wooded area. I could see grave yards and became hesitant when I saw a house that seemed to be sitting in the middle of the graveyard.

"Is that the house?" I asked.

"Yep," Tasha said.

We continued to drive past the graveyard when Tasha started to call out the name Joselyn.

"Joselyn, these are our cousins," she said.

"I don't see anybody." Danny said.

"Oh, she is buried right there," Tammy said as the other kids kept eating their candy. "She comes and plays in the room with us at night sometimes."

"What?" I asked as the truck stopped and they started getting off the truck.

"Yeah, it's OK, she just a ghost now, let's go watch Poltergeist."

Danny and I did not move. We grabbed each other's hand.

"MAMA!" we screamed.

"What's wrong?" she asked with concern.

"We walking home!"

2 THE TALES OF 2 SISTERS

"Tisha, when you get to the cookie jar, make sure you bring one for you and one for me, OK?" I said.

"OK, Lisa, and I'm going to be real quiet," she whispered as she climbed out of the bunkbed.

'I'm going to listen out for Mama for you."

"OK," she said.

Tisha quietly walked to the door and peeked out.

"Do you see Mama?" I asked.

"No," she said softly.

She started walking down the hallway towards the kitchen. I laid in bed and did not make a sound while listening for Mama. I looked at our window to see the moon casting a soft light into our room through our Raggedy Ann curtains.

As I lay, I began to hear what sounded like soft

squeaking sounds getting closer and closer to the room door. Tisha was walking to the door and every step I could hear the soft sounds.

"Tisha, what is that?" I asked.

"I gotta poot!" she said with her little girl attitude. "It wouldn't' stop coming out," she said.

"Ew!" I said as we both started laughing.

"Y'all gonna make me come in there and beat y'all butts! Go to sleep!" Mama yelled.

Tisha jumped in the bed with me. She never liked sleeping on the bottom bunk by herself, and I didn't like sleeping on the top. I was always scared the exorcist was going to come and get me from underneath the bed. We both continued to snicker as she handed me one of the cookies. She crawled to her end of the bed and I fell asleep at my end.

The next morning, I awakened to this awful feeling in my mouth. I opened my eyes to see Tisha's toes were in my mouth!

"Ew! Yuk!" I said, hitting Tisha.

"What?" Tisha said, still half asleep. "Mama, Lisa hitting me."

"Look, get y'all butts out the bed. The first

thing I don't want to hear this morning is y'all fussing," she said.

"Yes, ma'am," we said.

"We going to the country, so get your clothes on."

"Yes ma'am," we said.

We each took a bath and went to the kitchen to eat cereal. Mama was already dressed and ready for us to go.

"Come on," she said, and we raced out of the door.

"FRONT SEAT!" I yelled, racing Tisha to the car.

"No, I want to get in the front seat!" Tisha said.

"I'm the oldest," I said, making it to the car first. I opened the door and pulled the latch on the seat for the top to pop over enough for her to get in the back.

"Mama!" Tisha said. "I want to get in the front seat."

"You know what?" Mama said. "Both of y'all get in the back!"

"Aw man!" I said, mad at Tisha. "Move over," I told her as she smiled because I had to sit in the back seat too.

Mama pulled to the front of the store. "Come on," she said, getting out of the car.

We jumped between the seats and walked across the driver's seat.

"What are y'all heathens doing?" she said. "You don't walk across the seat, you pull the seat up and get out of the car," she said angrily. "Get two things and that's it."

We ran and got a drink and a pack of candy, then darted out the door. We watched as other cars pulled up and quickly got in the car and ducked down on the floor.

"Do you think they saw us?" I asked Tisha.

"No, we are going to keep hiding." Tisha said.

Mama came to the car fussing at us.

"You two are crazy. You want to buy things with food stamps, but you don't want anybody to see you use food stamps," she said.

We didn't say anything. We stayed on the floor holding our heads down so no one could see that she got in the car with us after using food stamps in the store.

"Y'all gonna drive me crazy, I forgot to get the gas," she said.

We pulled up to the gas pump and got out of the car. I peeked up to see if anyone was at the pump. We didn't care if we knew them or not, we didn't want anyone to know we had food stamps. I did not see anyone so I pulled the lever for the seat to pop up. Tisha got out of Mama's side of the care as I opened the door on my side.

"Mama, can I pump the gas?" I asked.

"Yes, Lisa," she said, sounding aggravated.

"I want to pump the gas, too," Tisha said.

"You're not old enough," I said.

"Uh huh!" she said.

"Nuh huh!" I said.

"Shut up! Both of you," Mama said. "Go ahead and pump the gas and get back in the car." Mama said walking back to the store.

I pulled the license plate down and opened the gas tank. I walked over to the pump and pulled the nozzle down, flipped the handle for the gas to turn on and once I heard what sounded like a little engine inside the pump, I knew it was ready for me to pump the gas.

I started walking to the back of the car to put the nozzle in the tank when Tisha started yelling.

"I want to pump! I want to pump!" she said.

"No! I'm pumping," I said.

We fought over the handle and, with my hand already ready to squeeze, the gas started pouring out of the nozzle.

"Ahh!" Tisha said as she started crying.

I stuck the nozzle in the tank and started to pump when I heard Mama coming out of the store.

"My eyes! My eyes!" Lisa said, crying as hard as she could.

"What did you do, Lisa?" Mama asked.

"She wouldn't let me pump the gas," I said as Mama picked Tisha up and rushed her to the water spigot on the outside of the store.

I took the nozzle out of the car and hung it back up, then ran over to where Mama and Tisha were. The store clerk and some other customers were with Mama and Tisha, too.

"Open your eyes, Tisha," Mama said. "I have to flush the gas out. Open your eyes."

Tisha kept crying, trying to open her eyes.

"Go in there and get me some milk," Mama told me.

"Some milk?" I said.

"Go get the milk!"

"I'll go get it," the store clerk said, rushing inside the store to get some milk. Mama kept trying to get the gas out. The clerk came with the milk and Mama poured the milk in her eyes.

"I'm going to get some towels," the store clerk said.

He went into the store and came out with a lot of towels for Mama to use on Tisha. Mama dried Tisha's face and asked her if she could see.

"Yes," she said, still crying.

Mama told us to go to the car and went back in the store to pay for the gas and milk. I opened the door for Tisha and this time, I didn't want to sit in front. I sat in the back with Tisha.

"OK, y'all, I'm going to work," Mama said.

"OK," we said, as we were used to being left alone, but today was different. We had our cousins with us and had a plan.

"Y'all ready to play welfare office?" I asked Tisha.

"Yup!" everyone said.

"We got to wait. Mama gonna come back to see what we are doing, so we can't start until she is gone."

Just like clockwork, Mama came back to see what we were doing and we were perfect little angels.

As soon as the coast was clear, we all scattered and started picking out sheets. We didn't have different color sheets so we pulled white sheets off the beds, out of the closet or wherever we could find them. We got chairs out of the kitchen and stood on them. We used thumbtacks to tack the sheets to the ceiling, creating dividers for each of our welfare offices.

We grabbed paper, pens, pencils, pencil sharpeners and stickers for our welfare offices. One of us worked at the food stamp office and the others just worked at which ever office came to mind.

We had so much fun, pretending to approve people for welfare and acting like 'adults'. We did not realize how much time had passed until we heard the door, which was also covered with a sheet, open and Mama start yelling.

"What in the world is going on?" she yelled. "Y'all got my house looking like the Ku Klux Klan in here! Get this mess down right now!"

We were all in shock that she caught us and started yanking down the sheets.

"Where did you get these sheets from?" she asked as she walked down the hallway. "Are y'all crazy! Get my sheets back on my bed!" she yelled.

We started putting everything back.

"Lisa and Tisha, I'm beating y'all butts," Mama said.

"Yes, ma'am," we said.

"That's OK, y'all. Tomorrow we will just play cops and prostitutes," I said.

"HUH?" our cousins said.

"Lisa, Tisha!" Mama shouted.

"Yes?" we answered.

"Get your butt up and get my kitchen clean," she said.

I looked outside to see it was pitch black and covered my head back up. All of a sudden, the covers were yanked off of me and a belt collided with my legs.

"Ouch!" I said.

"Get your butt up!" she said, yanking Tisha's cover off and striking her.

We both stumbled and walked into the kitchen. Tisha was crying and I refused to cry. I never wanted Mama to feel she got the best of me when I got a whipping so I would just hold it in like it didn't hurt.

We walked into the kitchen to see dishes piled, some not even cleaned before they were placed in the sink. I knew it had to be 2:00 a.m. or 3:00 a.m. and we had to go to school the next morning but that did not matter to Mama. If the kitchen wasn't cleaned when she got home, rain or shine, you got up to clean it.

I started running the dish water. There seemed to be more forks in the sink than anything. Tisha had a towel ready to rinse and dry.

"When I get out of this tub, this kitchen better be clean. I want to relax when I come home, eat my TV dinner and go to sleep," she said.

She opened the freezer and took her TV dinner out of the box and placed the foil divided dinner in the oven. She gave us a look of death and walked down the hallway towards the bathroom.

We washed the dishes and were down to the forks, spoons and knives. The forks seemed to be harder to clean so I looked down the hallway and back at Tisha who was busy drying the dishes and dropped the forks behind the stove.

"We done, come on." I said, heading to bed.

I laid back down, comfortable as can be. Then Tisha climbed in her bed and fell asleep. I dozed off into a deep sleep when I heard a screeching voice coming from the kitchen.

"Where is the world are all of my forks?" Mama shouted.

My eyes popped open as big as a quarter and I did not move.

"Oh lord!" I said. "She is gonna beat my butt."

~◇~

"Y'all get up and get ready for school," Mama said on the phone.

"Yes, ma'am," I replied.

I hung up the phone, thinking I could get a few more minutes of sleep. I laid back down and Tisha started pulling on my cover.

"Lisa! Lisa! I'm hungry," she said.

"Ugh. Ok, let's get ready for school," I said.

Tisha and I got ready for school, put on our book bags and went to the bus stop. We stood there looking and realizing no other kids were outside.

"We missed the bus," Tisha said.

"So," I said.

"Mama gonna be mad," Tisha said.

"Let's go back to the house," I said.

We went back in the house and Tisha started whining. "I'm hungry," she said.

I pulled out a box of cereal for her to eat.

"Tisha, we can't tell Mama we missed the bus," I said.

"But we did," she said.

"I know, but we can't tell her."

"I'm telling," Tisha said.

"Well, I'm not going to be your friend anymore," I said.

"Well, I won't tell if we play outside."

"OK. What do you want to play?" I asked.

"Let's race on our bikes."

"OK. We can race around the circle," I said, excited to go outside.

We took our bikes out and started riding. We started riding on our street, then branched out to the next street, then the entire neighborhood.

We decided to race around the house and as we raced, I realized Tisha wasn't behind me anymore. I turned around, calling her name, to see she had fell off her bike.

"I cut my moon off," she said, crying, referring to her breast.

"Your moon is cut off?" I asked.

"Yes," she said.

I took her in the house and could see the cut she had from her rusted handle bar. We put a bandage on it and went back outside, riding.

A mysterious car pulled up and we took off running to the house. We ran in the door and locked the door. I got a chair and Tisha helped me put it against the door. A knock came on the door.

"Lisa, Tisha, I just saw you," the voice said.

We didn't say a word.

"It's Ms. Jerry," she said.

"The principal!" we both said.

"Open the door."

"Ooo. We in trouble," Tisha said.

I moved the chair from the door, and standing at the door was Ms. Jerry.

"Where is your phone?" she asked.

"Right there," Tisha said, looking at the yellowish phone hanging from the wall.

"Call your mom, Lisa." she said.

I picked up the phone and called Mama. Ms. Jerry took the phone out of my hand.

"Hi, Ms. Jones. I'm here with Lisa and Tisha," she said.

A sound starting coming from the phone, sounding like screeching. Tisha and I looked at each other because we knew she was fussing.

"No, I'm not at the school. I saw them riding around the neighborhood on their bikes."

"THEIR BIKES!" I heard her yell clearly through the phone. The phone started making screeching sounds again.

"OK," Ms. Jerry, said hanging up the phone.

"Let's go," Ms. Jerry said.

We grabbed our book bags and walked out the door behind her. I grabbed the knob to make sure it was locked.

"I'm not getting into trouble with you," Tisha said.

"Yes, you are, or I'm going to snatch your other moon off," I said.

"What did you just say, Tisha?" Mama asked as we were riding in the back seat on our way to a Girl Scout meeting.

"How did she hear you?" I whispered to Tisha while chewing a piece of Juicy Fruit gum.

"I don't know," Tisha said.

"Because y'all don't know how to whisper. And Lisa stop smacking that gum!" Mama said. "You sound like a cow."

"Yes, ma'am," I said

"Do it," Tisha whispered to me.

"Do what?" Mama asked.

I reached over to Tisha and grabbed her head and leaned in as though I was going to whisper in her ear. At the same time, Mama adjusted the mirror so she could see in the back seat.

"Lisa, what are you doing?" she asked.

"She is going to spit in my ear." Tisha said.

"She is going to what?" Mama said as I sat back as quickly as I could. "Why is she spitting in your ear, Tisha?"

"It feels good, I spit in hers too," she said.

"Y'all about to be some nasty tail girls. Stop spitting in each other ears!" she said. "I can't believe I just had to say that," she said under her breath.

We arrived at the church where our Girl Scout meeting was held but had missed the meeting because we thought it was later than it was. There were still some of the children and adults lingering around talking to one another. Tisha and I decided that we would throw rocks to see which rock would go the furthest. I had Tisha stand by the church so I could throw the rock, but she didn't know I was aiming at her head.

"Are you ready?" I asked as she stood waiting.

"Yes," she said.

I threw the rock and I could see her running back and forth trying to avoid the rock, then it happened. Direct connection to her forehead. I stood looking at she hit the ground screaming and crying. Mama ran over to her with some of the adults and I could see blood everywhere.

I started running down to them and Mama was asking her what happened.

"We were throwing rocks," she said, still crying.

"Throwing rocks? What is wrong with y'all?" she said, picking Tisha up to take her to the car.

We took Tisha to the nearest Urgent Care where she received stitches in her forehead.

"Everywhere I ran, the rock seemed to follow me," she said.

"Lisa probably threw it on purpose," Mama said.

"Nuh uh!" I said, while thinking…is she on to me?

3 WHERE IS MY MAMA

It was Friday as my sister and I sat on the bus, unable to stay still, waiting to get home. We both knew exactly what to look for as soon as we got home. As the bus turned on our street we became more anxious, book bags in hand and we were ready to run as soon as the door opened.

The bus driver had one more stop before our house.

"We are almost there," I thought as the bus pulled up to the stop.

The bus driver decided to have a brief conversation with one of the parents which made our anxiety even more prevalent.

"Come on!" I said as they talked.

The conversation ended and we started riding again. As soon as the bus stopped and the door opened, we ran off the bus as fast as we could. When we got to the house, we knew we were not to go straight in. Mama taught us to walk the entire outside of the house first and make sure we didn't see any pried doors open or broken windows.

My sister Celia stayed at the front door while I walked, as fast as I could, around the house. She took the beaded key chain from under her shirt and unlocked the door. We both were almost knocking each other down trying to get inside the house.

"WOW!" Kim said, looking at the new clothes and shoes Mama had left on the couch for us.

"It's pretty," I said, picking a pink dress with ruffles.

We both had brand new shoes and clothes laid out on the couch. One end was her end and the other was mine. This was a routine that our mother had for us, every Friday, we got clothes and went to dinner for as far back as we could remember. Even though Celia was six and I was nine, she always got us at least one outfit alike to dress us as twins.

"I'm going to wear this Monday," Kim said.

"What is today?" I asked.

"Friday," Kim said.

"No, what day of the month?" I asked, walking over to the wall calendar.

"I'll wear mine in a week," I said.

"Why?" Kim asked.

"I don't wear new clothes on the first of the month, people will think we are on welfare and that's the only time we can afford to buy clothes, when the welfare checks come out," I said.

"But we not on welfare," she said.

"Yes, we are, we get food stamps," I said.

"Food stamps are not welfare," she said.

"Yes, it is."

"You can't buy clothes with food stamps, Kim."

"Just shut up, Celia," I said.

We both took our clothes to our room and placed them on the bed. We wanted everything to stay perfect and neat.

"I can't wait for Mama to get home so we can leave," Celia said.

"Me too, I'm hungry," I said.

"Do you want to wear matching outfits?" Celia asked.

"No, it's welfare time," I said.

"Please," she said, begging me to wear the

same outfit.

"OK," I said.

"Let's get ready for Mama when she get home."

"OK," I said as we both grabbed our outfits.

We ran into the room and started putting our clothes on. We knew Mama got home about an hour after we did so we wanted to be sure to be ready to go. We both ran into Mama's room to look in the big mirror she had to make sure we looked pretty.

We sat on the couch and became bored.

"Where is the wrench?" Celia asked.

"I'll do it," I said, walking to our floor model TV.

Our TV did not have a knob, only a white piece that was sticking out. We would typically use a wrench to turn it but it was gone.

"Is it on U?" Celia asked.

"Yeah, I'll get it," I said.

One of the knobs had to be on the letter U for us to get the channel we were looking for, and then we would turn the other. I used my fingers to turn the knob we needed for the channel and we could hear Mama outside talking to one of the neighbors.

I stopped trying to turn the TV and we ran to her as fast as we could.

"Mama!" we said. "Thank you, they are so pretty, are we going to dinner now?" we said over each other.

"Yes," she said. "Y'all about to knock me down."

"You two look so pretty, just like twins," our neighbor Ms. Sarah said.

"Thank you," we said, blushing.

"Let me go in here and get ready. I'll talk to you later, Sarah," Mama said.

"You all can stay out here if you want, just don't get dirty," she said, walking in the door.

"I don't want to play, let's go inside," I said.

"OK," Celia said.

We started walking towards the door and up the stairs.

"BOO!" Mama said. "Let's go," she said, laughing.

"I thought you wanted to get ready?" I said.

"I am ready and I am hungry!" she said. "Aren't y'all hungry?"

"Yes, ma'am," we said, racing to the car.

We finally made it home from dinner. Mama reached in the back seat of the car to pick up Celia who was sleeping.

"Did you have fun?" she asked.

"Yes," I said.

"Good."

"Can we watch TV?" I asked.

"OK, we have a little time before the TV shuts off for the night."

Mama and I laid on the couch watching television when Celia came and laid on the couch with us. We all feel asleep until we heard beeping coming from the TV set. I opened my eyes to see the normal striped image, notifying us that the channel was over for the night.

"We missed the National Anthem," Mama said, getting up off the couch. She turned off the TV and told us to go on to bed.

The next morning, we were up like clockwork. We already knew that we had to clean up. Cleaning up every Saturday morning was a ritual at our house. We did nothing at all until the entire house was clean. We swept, mopped, wiped down and everything so we had enough time to watch cartoons.

Mama would help us clean up and watch cartoons with us too sometimes, and this Saturday was one of the Saturdays she wanted to watch cartoons with us. As soon as we were close to being finished cleaning, she started breakfast so we could eat and watch cartoons.

I could smell the homemade pancakes from the back room and could not wait to sink my teeth in them. I could already see the cube of butter she would have on the top and the syrup dripping down the sides.

"Hurry up, Kim, I'm hungry," Celia said.

"Me, too," I said, hurrying.

We finished and ran up front to watch cartoons.

Mama gave us little trays to sit in front of us so we could put our food and drink on them while watching cartoons.

After cartoons were over we decided to have 'makeup' day with Mama. We ran in our room and got our strawberry, grape and cherry flavored lip gloss, earrings, rollers, combs, brushes and Kool Aid.

Mama sat on the floor and we stood behind her rolling her hair with big pink rollers. Some had little black pointing pieces coming out of them, the others had a pink clasp that gripped the hair. We brushed her hair, and put ear rings and lip gloss on her.

"What is the Kool Aid for?" Mama asked.

"We are going to dye your hair," I said.

"Oh no!" she said, laughing. "You can't dye my hair."

She played with us, tickling us and laughing. We were so happy to have a great weekend, just like all of our weekends. As night fell, she sent Celia to take a bath. She stood at a window looking out. I wasn't tall enough to see out the window, so I climbed on the couch to look too.

"Mama, how long are we going to live here?" I

asked.

"Forever," she said, never looking away from the outside.

"How long is forever?"

"Forever is forever, baby," she said.

"Until we die?" I asked.

"Yes, until we die," she said.

That Sunday, Mama told us to get dressed and get in the car.

"Where are we going?" Celia asked.

"It's a surprise," she said.

We drove for about an hour and half and could not figure out where we were going. Suddenly, in the tree line we saw a huge Ferris wheel.

"The fair!" I shouted.

"Yep, we are going to the State Fair," she said.

Celia and I were so excited. We could not believe we were at the State Fair. We couldn't get through the gate fast enough. As soon as we parked, we jumped out of the car hugging Mama.

"You are the bestest mama," Celia said.

"Aww, thank you," she said.

We rode rides, ate food, and played games until the fair closed. We climbed in the car with our prizes, candy apples, and cotton candy. We could not stop talking about how much fun we had the entire ride home. We got home and wanted to sleep with our mama so she let us climb in bed with her.

Monday morning came and off to school we went. We always shared the fun we had from the weekend on the bus with our friends. They always seemed just as excited as we did.

"Kim, let's make Mama some cards," Celia said.

"OK," I said, thinking about how happy she would be when she got the cards.

"We can make it when we get back home and hide it," she said.

"Why are we going to hide it, Celia?" I asked.

"Because when she surprises us with the clothes, we are going to surprise her with the cards."

"Yeah!" I said, smiling.

After a long day at school we both rushed home

to start working on the card before she came home. We checked the outside of the house quickly and ran in. We pulled out crayon, rulers, scissors, glue and even chalk from art class. We made designs and cut out pictures we drew of ourselves. As we were making the cards, we could hear her talking to the neighbor and rushed to hide everything under our mattress.

She came in and started to take her shoes off. We could see how tired she was but she still went into the kitchen and started cooking dinner.

"Tomorrow, we are going to cook for her," I told Celia.

"OK," Celia said.

We ate, took our baths and went to bed. Mama came in and turned on the light.

"You know what we haven't done in a while," she said.

Celia and I both sat up. "No, ma'am."

"We haven't said our prayers. We always fall to sleep," she said. "It is important to always say your prayers before bed," she said.

"OK," we said, getting out of bed.

She turned the light off and walked over to the bed and kneeled down. We knelt down beside her.

"Now I lay me down to sleep," she started and we joined.

"I pray the Lord my soul to keep. If I should die before I wake, I pray the Lord my soul to take."

"God bless Mama," I said.

"God bless Daddy, wherever he is," Celia said.

"God bless my two beautiful girls," Mama said.

"God bless you too, Mama," Celia and I said.

We climbed in bed and she kissed each of our foreheads.

The next morning, Celia and I woke up early and climbed on a chair to take chicken out of the freezer. We put the chicken under the sink so Mama wouldn't see the chicken.

Mama got up for work and out the door we went.

"Tonight we are going to make Mama some chicken, rice and peas and spaghetti," I said.

"OK," Celia.

We rushed the day along so we could make Mama her dinner. As soon as the bus dropped us off we rushed to check the outside and ran in the door. We pulled the chicken, which had unthawed and started to leak, from under the sink. We wanted to fry it but we were scared we would burn down the house so we put in the oven.

"What do we press?" Celia asked.

"I think she said she broil the chicken," I said. "Right there says broil."

I pushed the button so it could start broiling.

"Don't Mama wash the chicken?" Ceila asked.

"Oh, yeah," I said, looking for the soap. "Ceila, go to the bathroom and bring that bar of soap."

"OK," she said as she ran to the bathroom.

I pulled out the pot to put the chicken in and started taking it out of the wrap it was in. The chicken was heavy and slippery. I dropped it a few times before getting it in the sink. Celia came to the sink with the bar of soap and pulled a chair beside me. We washed the chicken, under the wings, in the inside and the legs.

"It's good as new now," I said.

"How do we cook spaghetti?" Celia said.

"Oh, we have to broil the noodles," I said.

I climbed on the counter to open the cabinet and grabbed the noodles. We opened the oven and poured the noodles on top of the chicken so they could broil.

"Kim, you have to get the rice and peas," Celia said.

"OK," I said, climbing back on the counter.

I picked out the rice and peas and turned the stove on.

"Don't you broil the rice and peas, too?" Celia asked.

"Yes, but I've seen Mama put the peas up here so I'm going to put the peas in the pot and pour the rice on it."

"OK," Celia said.

We put all the food on and ran to the room to start on the card again.

"Let's make the card in here so we won't have to rush if Mama comes home." I told Celia.

"OK," she said.

We started back coloring the card and cutting out designs when a smell of burnt food started reaching the room.

"What is that, Celia?" I asked as we both started running towards the kitchen. It was a little smoke forming and we could hear frying.

"What's wrong with our food?" Celia asked.

"I don't know," I said.

As soon as I reached for the pot I could hear Mama talking to the neighbor.

"Oh no, she is home and it is not done," I said.

"I'm going to hide the cards," Celia said, running back to the room.

As soon as she ran to the room, the fire detector went off. It scared me so bad I dropped the pot of peas and rice.

Mama rushed through the door screaming our names.

"Kim! Ceila!" she called, with Ms. Sarah right behind her.

I started crying.

"Kim, are you ok?" Mama asked.

"It was supposed to be a surprise," I said.

Ceila ran out of the room to me and we both cried together. Not only because we felt we ruined the surprise, but we thought we were in trouble.

"Aww, it's OK," Mama said, rushing to the smoke detector to fan it.

Ms. Sarah opened the oven to see a whole chicken with noodles burning at the top in the oven.

"What in the world is this, girls?" she asked.

"Spaghetti and chicken," we said.

Mama came in the kitchen and started laughing.

"Lord, I need to teach y'all how to cook," she said.

"You not mad?" Celia asked.

"No, I think this is cute, you tried to cook for me. Now let's go out to eat, I'm scared to eat that," she said, still laughing.

Friday morning came and we knew we would have our clothes but were even more excited that we had made cards for mama.

"Mama is going to be so happy," I said, waiting

at the bus stop.

"Yep, but we will never try and cook for her again," Celia said.

"Nope, never," I said.

The day went by as slowly as ever, but it was finally time to go home. We rushed to make sure the house was safe and ran in. Our clothes were on the couch, just like they always were. We had one matching outfit and two other outfits, and this time she added a necklace and earrings. We were so excited.

We took our clothes and put them in our room and got her cards from under the mattress. We sat one card on one side of the couch and one on the other.

"You want to watch TV until she comes?" Celia said.

"Yeah," I said.

I used my fingers to change the channel and we watched the wavy shows on the TV waiting for Mama.

We were laughing at the TV so much we did not realize it was night time.

"Kim," Celia said. "Where is Mama?"

I jumped off of the couch and ran to the door, thinking she was talking to the neighbor, but our car wasn't outside.

"I don't know," I said. "She is not home."

"What time is it?" Celia asked.

I went into the kitchen and saw it was almost 8:00 p.m.

"Celia, it's almost 8:00," I said. "Let's go to Ms. Sarah's house," I said.

We walked to Ms. Sarah house which was about two houses from our house and knocked on the door. There was no answer but we could hear voices whispering inside.

"Let's go," I said, grabbing Celia hand.

As we started walking away, the door opened.

"Come in, girls, I have been watching the house to make sure you are OK," she said. She looked like she had been crying a lot.

"Are you OK, Ms. Sarah?" I asked.

"Did you see your pretty clothes?" she asked.

"Yes, ma'am." I said. "Have you seen my Mama?"

"Did you see the earrings and necklace?"

"Yes, ma'am," Celia said.

As we were talking, a knock came on the door. Ms. Sarah got up to open the door.

"Auntie Joan!" Celia said.

"Hi, baby," she said.

"I haven't yet," Ms. Sarah said to Auntie Joan.

"Where is Mama, Auntie Joan?" I asked.

"Babies, I need you two to sit down," she said.

I knew in my gut something was wrong. I could tell because she looked like she had been crying too.

She began to cry without saying anything to us. I wiped one side of her face and Celia wiped another.

"Auntie," I said. "Where is my Mama?"

"Babies, your mama was killed in a car accident on her way home for lunch."

"No, she wasn't," I said. "She left our clothes and she had to come home to do that."

"I put them there," Ms. Sarah said.

"No, you didn't, my mama did," I said.

"I was on my way home and saw the accident. I ran to the car and held her hand waiting for the ambulance to come. She told me that it was very important for me to do something for her. She told me to tell you two she loved you and asked me to put the clothes on the couch for her."

"No, she is not dead!" I yelled. "Where is my Mama?"

"Baby, she died. I didn't know how to go over there and tell you so I called your aunt."

"I'm never going to see my Mama again?" Celia said.

"I'm never going to hold my Mama, or smell my Mama or kiss my Mama or touch my Mama?" Celia continued in complete shock.

"No, baby," Auntie Joan said, crying.

Celia started to cry. I held on to Celia but did not cry. I still did not believe she was dead.

"Let's get some clothes so you can come to my house," Auntie Joan said.

"I'm staying home and waiting for Mama," I

said, letting go of Celia's hand and storming out of the door.

Auntie Joan, Celia and Ms. Sarah came after me as I started running home.

"Mama! Mama!" I screamed, running through the house. "Mama! Please answer me."

Auntie Joan, Celia and Ms. Sarah came in the door. They were all crying.

"Mama, where are you? I need to smell you, I need to hold you, Mama. I have to play in your hair and put lip-gloss on you," I said. "I have to hear your voice, Mama, I know you are somewhere, where are you?"

I ran to the couch and grabbed the cards.

"Look, Mama we made you a surprise, we made you cards because we love you. Mama, please answer me!" I yelled. "Mama, we have to go to dinner tonight and watch cartoons tomorrow, you have to say prayers with us tonight, Mama. Where are you? I need to see your face!"

I constantly screamed for her at the top of my lungs.

"Mama! You cannot leave me, Mama, where are you?" I yelled.

Finally, I broke down crying because I knew they were telling me the truth. Mama would have never let us be home by ourselves at night, Mama would have never not answered me. Mama would have always been right there for us, Mama would not have let us cry. I knew she was gone.

Celia ran to me and hugged me.

"We don't have a mama anymore," Celia said, crying. "We don't have a mama anymore."

"We have each other, Celia," I said, crying uncontrollably. "We still have each other."

4 DOWN SOUTH

"What is that smell?" I heard Martin say as I started to smell an awful smell too.

We both covered out noses to a smell that smelled like someone had did number two and started cooking it.

"You pooted?" I said to Martin.

"No, you did," he replied.

"That's pig feces," Mama said, laughing.

"Pig what?" I asked.

"It's that plant right there, they use pig poop to fertilize the soil."

"They use who to do what?" Martin said.

We popped our head out the car window to see a long silver building, with what looked like water sprinklers shooting water all over the grass.

"Mama," I said through my hands, "what the water sprinklers for?"

"That's not water," she said, laughing.

"It's not?" Martin and I asked, looking at each other with our hands still over our nose and mouth.

"Are we almost there?" Martin asked.

"Almost," she said. "We will get there before dark."

Mama turned down a road that took us past the building and soon the smell started to go away.

"Where is she taking us?" I asked.

"She said Aunt Virginia's house," Martin said.

"Well, where does she live, on Pluto?" I said as we both laughed.

"Look, Lorena," Martin said. "There are cows right there."

"Real cows?" I said, rushing to his side of the car. "I've never seen cows in real life before."

"Me either," Martin said.

"They have cotton fields, corn fields, cabbage, a lot of different fields"

"Really?" we said in amusement.

"Yes," she said.

"Keep looking, you will see more cows, horses, and pigs too."

"Wow," we said, with our faces hanging out of the window, looking at everything that passed.

We kept driving and there weren't very many houses to see, only land, a house here or there, fields and animals. Mama would tell us what type of field we were passing each time we passed one. We thought she was the smartest person in the world to look at the rows of what we thought was nothing and tell us what type of food it was.

"Mama, how do you know what it is?" I asked.

"I grew up down here."

"Mama, were you a slave?" Martin asked.

"No," she said, laughing. "We own a lot of this land."

We pulled up to a big white house. It was so big to us. We could see a few trailers in the distances.

"We're here," she said.

"WOW! This is a big house," I said.

"It's not that big," Mama said, as a bunch of kids ran out of the house.

They were all happy and hugging us. We were confused because we didn't know any of them.

"These are your cousins," Mama said.

"Y'all come on inside," one of the kids said, grabbing my hand.

Martin and I ran up the stairs and into the house and it was beautiful. It had hard wooden floors, off-white walls, old pictures, some hanging crooked on the walls and a big thing in the middle of the floor with fire inside of it.

The house smelled like a mix of wood, fire, fresh biscuits and bacon. There was a hint of sweetness in the air. It was a smell I had never smelled before, but I knew from that moment it would be one I would never forget.

As I walked through the living room, I couldn't help but notice brown strips hanging from the ceiling. As I gazed at the strips, I could see my mom out of the corner of my eye looking my way.

"That's a fly strip," Mama said.

"Eww, so those are dead flies?" I said.

"Yes."

I continued my voyage to look around the

house and peaked in a room to see a big bed with flower print covers, buckets of water and slippers on the floor.

"Lorena?" a woman said as she popped from around the corner, scaring me.

I looked up to see a stout woman with a pretty brown round face. She wore glasses and a big flower printed gown with pockets.

"Yes, ma'am," I said.

"You got big, child," she said with a deep country accent.

"That's your aunt Virginia," Mama said.

"Where is Martin?" she asked.

"He is somewhere with the kids," Mama said.

Being inquisitive, I wanted to look around the house. I walked near the thing in the middle of the floor and stared at it. It had a pot on the top and I could see the fire through a little glass window.

"Mama," I asked. "What is this?"

"That's the stove," she said.

I stood, confused, looking at this odd shaped object not understanding how it could be the stove.

Our stove wasn't in the middle of the floor and it had a switch that ticked before the flames came on. This was nothing like a stove I had seen before.

"It's a wooden stove, they put wood in it and the fire is used to cook and heat the house up too," Mama said.

"Oh, OK," I said, still staring at it. I was amazed at how it looked and to know what it was made me even more amazed.

I looked across the kitchen to see flour, eggs, vanilla flavoring, iron pots and pans—some with handles, many without—pot holders, wash cloths and drying towels in the kitchen.

"Lorena, we are going to our other cousin's house. Come on," Martin said.

"OK," I said, running out of the door behind him.

We ran across a grassy area to a long trailer. I had only seen trailers as we passed them on the highway. I never gave it a second thought of how the inside looked until we got to the trailer.

One of the kids walked up to the door and opened it and I was surprised to see it looked like a little house. I walked up the little stairs and through the door. They had a living room, bedroom, and a kitchen. The walls were brown with black lines, and it seemed like everything in the trailer was brown.

The adults were drinking beer and playing "Second Time Around" by Shalamar. They were laughing, talking, and completely ignoring us as we ran through the house.

We went into one of the rooms of the house. On a built in dresser were two blue "The Bible Story" books.

"You want to play?" one of my cousins said.

"Sure," I said. "What is your name?"

"Oh, I'm Rose, that's Paul, and James," she said.

"Oh, OK. I'm Lorena and that's Martin. I have a Slinky."

"What's a Slinky?" they all said.

I pulled out my Slinky and clackers to show them.

"What are those?"

"That's a Slinky and clacker. You haven't seen these?" Martin said.

"No," one of my cousins said.

"I have a snake," Paul said.

"A snake!" Martin and I said.

"Yes, here," he said, picking up a toy snake off the floor. "If you hold the tail, the head will move by itself."

"Aye y'all, get from 'round there, we going to the juke joint. Come on now," we heard.

"Y'all come on, we going back to Aunt Virginia's house."

Martin and I started to go to the front of the trailer when Paul told us to follow him. He opened a back door and it was dark outside. There were no lights anywhere, just pitch black. They started jumping out the door, not stepping on any of the steps at the back door, so we did too.

We made sure not to lose sight of them because we had no idea how to get back to Aunt Virginia's house. Once we got there, we walked in and all the kids went into one room.

I wanted to be nosey because I was smelling food. I could still smell the bacon. But I saw different cakes on the counter, a big bucket on the floor and an old pan, looking like they were ready to put food in to cook.

"Mama," I said. "Why is she cooking bacon for dinner?"

"That's not bacon, that's fat back," Mama said.

"Mama?" I asked. "She is cooking the fat out of people's back?"

"No," she said, laughing, "It's kind of like a salty bacon. She uses it to cook in greens for flavor."

"Oh," I said, with a little confusion.

"Y'all go back there and get me some peas," Aunt Virginia said.

"OK," the kids said. "Y'all come on."

They started running towards the back of the house.

"Y'all better stop running in here. You make my cakes fall, I'm going to beat y'all butts," Aunt Virginia said.

We walked fast past a little opening to a spring door.

"The cakes fall off the table?" I asked Rose.

"No, the ones in the oven will fall," she said.

"Fall?" Martin asked.

"Into the fire?" I asked.

"No, the middle will cave in and then the cake is bad. Aunt Virginia will get mad if it falls."

"Oh, OK," we said, walking out the door.

It was dark; you couldn't see anything except the area that was shining from in the house onto the trees in the back yard. Paul cut the porch light on and it lit up the rest of the trees.

"Let's go," they said, as they started running towards the woods.

We ran after them and they went straight into the woods. We stopped. We could see the path they went down but we didn't see the lights of a store.

"I'm not going in there," I told Martin.

"Me, either. I wonder how far the store is in there."

We went back to the porch and sat on the stairs waiting for them to come back. We heard dogs, birds, crickets and sounds we had never heard. The longer we waited, the more we became scared.

Out of the blue, we could see them running back.

"Where did y'all go?" James asked, with the bottom of his shirt full of peas.

We noticed all of them had peas in their shirts.

"We didn't see the store," Martin said.

"The store?" they said, walking past us to the house.

We walked in behind them and they dumped all the peas in the bucket that was in the kitchen.

"They didn't give you a bag to put those in?" I asked.

"What y'all talking about?" Aunt Virginia asked.

"When they went to the store for the peas," I said.

"There ain't no store back there, the field back there, you pick 'em fresh," she said.

"Y'all scaredy cats," James said, laughing.

"Get me some water," Aunt Virginia said. "And not out my room."

"Y'all come on," Rose said, grabbing a pot.

James and Paul grabbed a pot so we did too.

"Why are y'all going outside? Where is the sink?" I said.

"We don't got no sink we get the water from outside," Paul said.

"Outside?" Martin and I said.

"Cut that light on," James said.

Paul turned on the porch light and we started following them. They walked almost to the middle of the yard and there was this black looking lever with a pipe. It was surely something we had never seen before.

James started to lift the lever as Rose put the pot under it. When he pushed down, water came out of it.

"Whoah!" Martin and I said.

"Y'all ain't never seen this here before?" James said.

"No," we said.

I was fascinated by it. I couldn't not understand how water came out of it and my mind immediately went to wanting to play with the lever.

We each filled out pots and took them back to the house. Aunt Virginia was sitting on a chair with the bucket with the peas in it between her legs. She would take one out, crack it and run her fingers down the center. I was staring so hard she noticed and started laughing.

"You ain't never seen anyone shell peas befo'? she said.

"No, ma'am." I said.

"Shirley, what are you teaching these kids?" Aunt Virginia said.

"How to go to the store and pick up a pack of peas," Mama said, laughing.

"Mama, I have to go to the bathroom." I said.

"Rose, go on and show her where the bathroom is," Aunt Virginia said. "This 'otta be fun."

"OK," Rose said.

"I have to go too," Martin said.

"OK, let's all go."

"Let's all go to the bathroom?" I said.

"Yeah. We might as well since we will all be there anyway."

We headed to the front door.

"Wait," I said. "Where is the bathroom?"

"It's outside," James said.

"Outside?" Martin and I asked.

"Ha!" Aunt Virginia said. "This 'otta be good, go on out there with y'all uppity city tail, go to the bathroom," she continued as she started laughing.

"This one has a little light from the pole, you can see inside when you open the door, but it's gonna be dark when you close it," Rose said.

I didn't say anything. I felt Martin grab my hand as we walked up to what was a little box. Rose opened the door and a smell from the dark ages came out. I looked in the toilet and saw it full of maggots.

"Ahh!" I screamed and took off running back to the house.

"Get me out of here! Get me out of here!" I cried, running back to the house.

I ran straight to Mama and hugged her. The kids started coming in laughing with Martin not far behind yelling.

"Y'all OK?" Aunt Virginia said, laughing. "You may need to take these little rich kids to the sto' to the bathroom."

"We not rich, Aunt Virginia," Mama said, trying herself not to laugh. "They just not used to the country."

"I need to stop by Jesse's house anyway so I'll go over there and come right back," Mama said.

"Oh, OK, dinner will be done directly," Aunt Virginia said.

We got in the car and Mama drove about a mile down the road to her cousin Jesse's house. We got out, but Jesse wasn't home.

"Y'all gonna have to go back in the outhouse," Mama said.

"Is that what that thing is called?" Martin said.

"Yes."

"Mama, why can't we just pee out here like we do when we traveling? You can open the door, we can pee and get back in," I said.

"OK," she said.

We headed on back to Aunt Virginia's house and although I did not like the outhouse, I still loved the sight of her home. We went inside and everything was just about done. Our cousins were helping with the peas.

"Can I help with the peas?" I asked aunt Virginia.

"You sho?" she asked. "You not gonna run if you see a worm, now are ya?" she said, laughing.

"A worm?" I said.

She started to laugh. "If you want to help, come on."

I noticed that there was a pot with peas sitting in water.

"What are those for?" I asked.

"Oh, I soak them first, these are not for tonight. I'll cook 'em tomorrow."

"Ohhh, OK," I said.

We finished the peas and Mama was taking out all of the other foods. Aunt Virginia grabbed some plates and forks and started serving plates. I had not seen so much food on one plate in my life. We had baked and fried chicken, fried fish, fried pork chops, potato salad, macaroni and cheese, field peas, rice and gravy and collard greens. For dessert we had pound cake, lemon meringue pie, and pecan pie.

"Mama, is it Thanksgiving?" I asked.

"No, it ain't Thanksgiving," she said.

"No, baby, this is how us country folk eat," Aunt Virginia said smiling.

We sat down to eat and my mouth had not ever tasted food so rich, so moist and so delicious. All the flavors, although we had them in the city, tasted much different. The spices were stronger and the food was popping with flavor. The cakes tasted like butter when you bit into it, it just melted. I could not stop eating.

"Slow down, Lorena, you're going to hurt yourself," Aunt Virginia said, laughing.

"It's so good," I said.

"Um hum," Martin said, asking for seconds.

I wanted to eat more and more but my stomach could not hold it.

"Well, I'm glad y'all like it," she said.

"It's delicious, Aunt Virginia."

"Mama," Martin said, "your food is good but this food is gooder."

"Gooder?" I said, laughing.

"Yeah. Gooder because it's better than better," he said.

Mama looked at us and laughed as we sat in obvious discomfort from eating so much food.

"Shirley, you need to bring these kids here more often so they can eat. They skin and bones," Aunt Virginia said.

"Hush," Mama said, laughing. "You all need to hurry up so you can wash up and go to bed, we have church tomorrow."

"Church?" Martin said.

"Yes, church," Mama said, popping him in the back of the head.

Mama sent us to a back room to unpack our clothes and look for our pajamas. She stayed in the kitchen and helped Aunt Virginia wash the dishes. I stood in the door as they used a big pot full of water to wash and rinse the dishes. Although they did not have running water, I found it amazing how the Southerners were so comfortable with not having basic utilities like we did in the North.

As force of habit, I was looking for a shower to wash. I had my pajamas, towel, wash cloth, soap, toothbrush and toothpaste and walked into the kitchen to Mama.

"Mama, where is the shower?" I asked.

"Shower?" Aunt Virginia said, laughing. "You know that outhouse you probably ran from?"

"Yes, ma'am," I said.

"There's your shower," she said, laughing.

I stood frozen in my spot, not understanding what she meant.

"Baby, we have to get a bucket and go out there and wash."

"Never mind," I said and walked back in the room.

"Y'all city folk," I could hear Aunt Virginia say, laughing at me as I walked in the room.

I put my pajamas on and crawled inside of the fluffy bed with a thick quilt. Martin was already sleep and had not even taken his clothes off. Mama came in the room and grabbed her towel.

"Come on, Lorena, I will go out there with you," she said.

"No, ma'am, it's dark, it smells and it has maggots in the toilet," I said.

"OK, I will get some water from outside and

we can just wash in here," she said.

"OK, I'll go outside with you," I said.

We walked outside and it was pitch black. You could hear animals and bugs but couldn't see anything for miles outside of the light shining from the porch. Mama walked to the well and put the bucket underneath and I pumped the water. Although it was nothing I was used to, something about the down South was so beautiful to me.

We went back inside and I grabbed my washcloth to wash my face. I dipped the cloth in the water and it was cool.

"Mama," I said.

"We would have to put it on the stove to warm it up," she said.

"Oh, OK, never mind," I said.

I began to wash myself with the cool water and although it wasn't the best feeling, I was actually enjoying the experience of something I had never experienced before.

I climbed back in the bed and covered up. There were no TV's, no cars, no radios blaring, none of the sounds I was used to in the city. It was the most peaceful sound I had heard...silence.

I was awakened by the sounds of roosters crowing, kids running and the smell of fresh bacon and biscuits. I looked around and noticed there was barely any daylight outside. It seemed to still be dark.

"Why does the rooster crow so late at night?" I thought. "And why are they kids out there running?"

I looked to see Mama and Martin still asleep. I eased out of bed and walked to the door. Rose was walking in with eggs in her shirt and Paul had a bucket of water.

"I see sleeping beauty has woken up," Aunt Virginia said as she passed the door. "Your mama and brother gonna let the whole day pass by and miss it."

"What time is it?" I asked.

"It's already almost 6:00," she said.

"At night?" I asked.

"Lord no, baby, in the morning. What time do

you get up at home?" she asked.

"Well, it depends." I said. "Sometimes 9:00, sometimes 10:00, but if it's Saturday we get up early so we can watch cartoons."

"Cartoons?" Aunt Virginia said, laughing. "Well, these babies get up early so we can have milk, eggs, and food to eat."

"Where do they get the milk from?" I asked.

"The cows out back," she said.

"You have cows?"

"Oh yes, I have cows, pigs, and chickens," she said. "John goes to the lake and catch fish when we want fish."

"Oh wow," I said in amazement.

"You ask a lot of questions. Do you like it here?"

"Yes ma'am, I think it's beautiful here. Everything except the bathroom is beautiful," I said.

Aunt Virginia laughed. "Well, I misjudged you sweetheart. I thought you didn't like it here," she said.

"Can I see the cows?" I asked.

"Sure, get your cousins to show you where they are. They are outside," she said. "Hurry up because you have to get ready for church."

"OK." I said, as I ran in the room to change my clothes.

I started out the door and realized I had to go to the bathroom but wanted to wait just a little longer for more daylight.

"Rose! Rose!" I yelled as I stood on the porch.

I did not hear her answer so I went back in the house and out of the back door.

"Rose!" I yelled.

"Yeah," I heard coming from the woods behind the house.

I ran off the porch towards the woods and saw Rose and Paul coming from the woods.

"Can you take me to see the cows?" I asked.

"Yeah, come on," she said, running back towards the woods.

I ran with them a little more comfortable than I was the night before because daylight was coming up rather quickly. We ran down a trail that had nothing but dirt and trees and they seemed to be able to navigate through it as if it were open highway.

All of a sudden, we ran upon an open field. It was huge! I saw rows of plants that I thought could have been food, pigs, cows, chicken, hens, roosters and even cats and dogs. I was amazed. James was sitting on a chair with buckets milking one of the cows.

"Wow!" I said.

"You ain't never seen nothing like this befo'," Rose said.

"No." I said.

"Aunt Donna has some sheep at her house."

"Wow," I said.

I gazed at what appeared to be endless land, animals and nature. The sun sky was getting lighter and lighter as I watched the animals roam across the land and Paul lay down seeds.

"You want to help me get some eggs?" Rose asked.

"Sure," I said as we started to run towards two handmade houses that chickens were walking in and out of.

The smell wasn't as bad as I thought it would be. There were boards and hay all over the floor, little pellets and boxes.

"What are the boxes for?" I asked.

"Oh, that's for nesting."

"Ohh," I said.

"Rose, I have to run to the bathroom." I said.

"We all have to go in anyway, it's almost time to eat and go to church."

"How do you know it's almost time?" I asked.

"When you live down here, you don't have to really look at the clock, the sky will tell you everything," she said.

I looked up at the sky which was a soft blue but saw nothing but the peeking of daytime.

Rose walked with me to the outhouse and by the time we got there, the sky was completely lit. I was happy to be able to see inside of the outhouse better than I could the night before. I walked to the door and when I opened it, an odor of death greeted me.

"Ew!" I said holding my nose. I stepped in to see maggots all over the toilet and it filled with brown feces.

"I'm going to be sick," I said, gagging.

"Lorena, go behind the outhouse then. I'll get you some tissue."

"OK," I said, walking around the back of the outhouse. I knew I couldn't hold it any longer but I knew I was not going to go inside of the outhouse.

We got back to the house, sat down for breakfast and everyone took turns washing up for church. I heard Aunt Virginia ask Mama to take some food to the car. I was confused as to why would we take food to church.

We put our church clothes on and we headed to church. The car was so crowded, we were sitting in each other's lap. After we got to the church, I got out to see a brick building with a steeple. Our church in the city was inside a big building that looked like a warehouse.

We walked in and the ushers, all dressed in white, handed us a fan. They escorted us to an area to sit in the church. We all sat on a long wooden chair that had Bibles and Hymn books sticking out of the back of the chair in front of us.

We listened to the choir sing, which was a singing I had never heard in the city. The sounds that came from their voices was full of soul…real soul. It sounded as if they were reaching into our bodies with their words. Some of the songs they sang with musical instruments, others the church stomped their feet on the ground to create the beat. It was the most amazing experience I had ever had.

After the choir sang songs, an older woman got up and read the announcements for the church upcoming events. They then sent around small round bowls for an offering.

I noticed a man and wife were sitting in chairs that looked like it were for a king and queen.

"Who is that?" I asked mama.

"That's the preacher and his wife," she said.

"Shh," Rose said as Mama handed me and Martin a piece of peppermint candy.

Shortly after the offering and after the choir sang again, the preacher got up. His voice was big and loud. He sounded as if he was singing sometimes, yelling some times and sometimes speaking a total different language. I was confused as to why people were jumping up, screaming, falling on the floor. Some people had towels over their legs while others fanned them. Some ran around the church as the organ played faster and faster. I had no idea what was going on besides hearing whispers of 'The Spirit and The Holy Ghost.' All I knew at that point was, I didn't know whether to sit still or run. Although there was what seemed to be chaos, there was a calm, a rejoicing and a family-hood. One like I had never seen before.

"Reach across the aisle and grab a neighbor," the pastor said.

People started hugging family, friends and even people they did not know like me and Martin.

"Say neighbor," the pastor said.

"Neighbor," everyone repeated.

"I love you," the pastor said.

"I love you," everyone repeated.

"And I am here," the pastor said.

"And I am here," everyone repeated.

"Because of His mercy," the pastor said.

"Because of His mercy," everyone repeated.

"Now give the Lord some praise," the pastor said as people clapped, danced in their spots, held their hands to the sky or closed their eyes rocking back and forth mumbling to themselves.

Four hours after we arrived at the church I heard the pastor say join hands. He said another prayer as everyone held hands.

"All hearts and mind clear?" he asked. "Let the church say Amen," he said.

"Amen," the church said and everyone dismissed as if it were the end of the school day.

Martin and I started walking towards the door when Paul, James and Rose told us to come downstairs.

"They have a downstairs?" I asked.

"Y'all come on," Mama and Aunt Virginia said.

We followed them down some narrow steps to an area that had a kitchen, chairs and tables of food. Kids were running around playing, people were talking, and it seemed as if the entire church was down there as one big family. It was yet another addition to the amazement I had encountered so far.

My cousins and I went outside and played with the other kids from the church. We picked up and threw rocks on the dirt road. It was so much fun until I heard those words.

"Lorena! Martin! Let's go!"

"Aww man!" I said as Rose, Paul and James started walking to the front of the church, where we could hear Mama calling us.

"Come on," I said to my cousins.

"We are getting ready to go back home," Mama said.

"Huh?" I said. "Now?"

"Yes, I have to go to work tomorrow."

My heart dropped, I did not want to leave. I wanted to cry but I didn't want them to see me cry.

"How are they going to get back home?" I asked.

"Baby, this is where they live, Aunt Virginia will be here until tonight with the church," Mama said.

"We have to get our stuff," Martin said.

"It's in the trunk. We have to go, so come on," she said.

"We will see you next time you come, OK?" Rose said.

"OK," I said as we gave each other a hug.

"Bye, Paul. Bye, James," Martin said as he got in the car.

"Bye," they said as I walked to the car holding back tears.

I got in the car and got on my knees in the back seat so I could look out. I started to cry and wave goodbye to them as we drove off. I would not stop looking out of the window. I wanted to see every tree, every dirt road and every animal. As we were leaving, we passed the big white house of Aunt Virginia. I looked at the outhouse and well and thought to myself how the experience of Down South would be one that I would never forget.

5 WHERE'S MY DAD

"Dad is coming to see me, Mommy," I said as I hung up the payphone.

"He is?" Mommy asked.

"Yep, that's what he just told me. And guess what?" I said.

"What?" she asked.

"I can show my friends my dad when he gets here."

"That's great!" she said.

We were walking back home on a scorching hot day, but the heat did not bother me. I was happy! Happy I could see my dad. I walked as fast as I could, hearing her behind me telling me to slow down. I could not wait to rush in the door and pick out the prettiest little dress I could wear for my dad.

Once we got home, I ran to my room.

"There it is," I said, finding the pretty dress I

had in mind on my long walk home.

I looked in my drawer and picked out my stockings, went to my closet and picked out my black Barbie doll shoes and ribbons for my hair. I was so excited to see my dad I could hardly sit still. I had not seen him since I was…well, I don't remember how old I was.

"Staci," I heard my mom call.

"Yes, ma'am," I said.

"Come here."

I walked into the living room with my ribbons in hand, smiling.

"When is your dad supposed to come visit you?" she asked.

"He said soon, Mommy."

"Hmm. I want you to put your ribbons back up."

"No Mommy, he is coming this time," I said.

"I didn't say he wasn't coming. I don't want you to mess them up, OK?" she said.

"Oh, OK. I'll put them in my special drawer."

As I was laying my clothes on the bed as neat as I could, I heard someone knock on the door.

"Who is it?" Mommy asked.

"Can Staci come out?" I heard.

I dropped everything and ran to the door with excitement to tell them my dad was coming to see me. I took off running, nearly knocking down my mommy.

"Slow down!" Mommy said as I ran past her out the door.

"My dad is coming to see me," I said to my friends.

"Really? We have never seen your dad before," my friend Rachel said. "We only see Traci's dad."

"Oh, mine is tall, and really nice," I said, using only my imagination because I had no memory of what he looked like. "He is going to play with me, take me places, buy things for me and we are going to have fun!" I said.

"Yayyy!" Rachel said, grabbing my hand with my other friends as we all jumped around in a circle, celebrating my dad coming to see me.

A week went by and no dad.

"Mommy, can we go call dad? Maybe he got lost," I said.

"OK," she said and we started walking to the store. It was hot with little raindrops in between. I didn't even think about the raindrops. I wanted to get to the phone so I could make sure my dad was OK.

We finally made it to the payphone and my mom stuck a dime in to make the call. She stood there for about a minute and hung up.

"Mommy, why did you hang up?" I asked.

"There is no answer." she said.

"Call him again, mommy, please," I said.

"OK," she said, putting the money in the phone to call again.

 She stood quietly again and I knew that he had not answered. I dropped my head and started to walk away.

"Staci!" she called. "Staci!" she called again as I continued to walk away.

Mommy caught up with me as I was walking because I started walking slower and slower. I wanted to go home, stay there and not do anything.

I just wanted to cry.

"Let's go to McDonald's and get an ice cream cone," Mommy said once she caught up.

"I just want to go to go home," I said as I started to cry.

"Staci, don't cry, you will have a great summer," Mama said as I continued to cry.

"Help me!" I said as I ran as fast as I could.

Everyone was laughing at me as I nearly lost my breath running around the house.

"Don't let him catch me!" I said, nearly crying running. I wouldn't dare look behind me because I knew he was back there chasing me.

I turned the corner and BAM, there he was. My stepdad standing looking at me with a big grin. I stood in horror as he was looking down at me laughing, all gums and his teeth in his hand.

I screamed and ran the other way. Everyone continued to laugh at me as they knew I was terrified of his teeth not being in his mouth.

"Stop! Stop! Help me!" I screamed, still running. Finally the laughing at me was over, his teeth were back in his mouth and I was tired and worn out from running.

"You are such a little girl," my sister Traci said to me.

"Shut up," I said, still gasping for air.

"Come on," he said in his West Indian accent, getting into his big beautiful maroon and gray Astro Van.

We hopped in the van and looked through the blinds as we drove around the city. He was fussing at the cars in road rage.

"Move, you meatball!" he shouted as he blew his horn.

We laughed as we heard horns blowing back at us and other people on the road. We rocked back and forth from the large and small potholes in the road as we rode. Each street light we approached, we would count how many seconds before on all the blocks ahead lights would turn either red or green at the same time. We watched the water beneath us as we crossed big bridges.

We arrived at the store and Daddy opened the door for us to get out. As soon as the door opened we heard music from a store next to the store we were going into.

"I want to get a record," I said to my sister Traci, looking at the LPs and 45s hanging from the store windows.

As I looked, I could imagine the smell of the record covers as I looked through the records. Music was a passion of mine, which was one of the reasons the store captivated me as soon as I heard the music.

"I want to get a record, a TV, boom box and a dookie chain," she said.

"Yup, just like Salt-N-Pepa," I said as we both laughed.

We walked inside the store. All we could see was a massive clutter of clothes and shoes. This was heaven to us.

"Alright. Staci and Traci," Daddy said. "Get some play and school clothes."

We sprinted through the store, picking up acid washed jeans, Wendy's "Where's the Beef" T-shirts, Pumas, and our favorite, Kangaroo sneakers with pockets on the side.

"I'm going to put money in here," I said.

"Me too." Traci said.

We picked up little girl training bras and underwear that had the days of the week on them. Neither one of us needed training bras but we knew we would just put tissue or egg carton bottoms in them to pretend we did need them.

We raced to the register for Daddy to pay for our clothes, comparing the clothes we had chosen. We bragged about how excited we were to get back to school from the summer to compare our new clothes with our classmates.

"Come now," he said signaling, that he was ready to go.

We ran to the van, excited about our new clothes. We could not wait to get home and take everything back out again so we could look at them and try them on again.

We got home and ran straight into our room, digging through our bags. We were excited because we wanted to wear some of our clothes at the block party we were having on our street that day. We picked out our outfits and out the door we went.

Summer went by fast, but the memories of the block parties, amusement parks, and trips out of the country were etched in our minds. As we headed home, we talked about all of the excitement we had when we were gone.

We enjoyed our summer with block parties, amusement parks, trips out to the country, and excitement. It was always exciting to be with my stepdad. He never treated me any different than Traci; he treated us the same.

"What did you do this summer?" Rachel said.

"We had fun!" I said with excitement. "My daddy came and got us and we had so much fun!"

"He is not your daddy, he is Traci's dad," Rachel said.

"He is mine, too!" I said, becoming angry.

"Don't get mad, Staci," Rachael said. "But, when is your dad coming?"

"He's not," I said. I started to feel like crying as soon as I said it.

"I knew your dad wasn't coming, Staci, he never comes here," my friend Vanessa said.

"Shut up! You're not my friend. I HATE Y'ALL!" I said, crying and running home.

I ran in the house to my room and cried on the

bed.

"I hate you, I hate you!" I said, crying as hard as I could.

"Staci?" Mommy said, coming in the room. "What's the matter?"

"I hate him, Mommy, why didn't he come see me?" I asked, crying.

"Well, maybe he was waiting for your birthday. It is in a couple of weeks," Mommy said.

"Can we go call him?" I asked.

I could tell by the look on her face that she really did not want to go, but she said yes anyway.

"OK, let's go," she said.

The closer we got to the phone, the more anxious I became. I started to play the scenario of what I thought would happen in my mind.

"Hi, Dad," I say.

"Hi. baby girl," he says.

"Are you coming to see me?"

"Absolutely. I will be there Friday night. No worries, I'll be right there."

"OK, Dad. I love you."

"I love you too, baby girl."

I smiled as my mind became happy with what I thought would happen. My steps started to pick up as I got closer to the phone.

We finally reached the phone and Mommy puts the dime in and I began to get excited.

"Hello, Staci wants to talk to you," she says.

The excitement filled my body because he answered. I could not believe he answered.

"Hi, dad!" I said with excitement.

"Hi, baby girl," he said.

"Are you coming to see me?" I asked.

"I'm sorry, baby girl, I can't come."

"Why?"

"I'm working so much. I just have a lot of work to do."

"My birthday is coming soon. Are you going to send me a card?"

"I don't have any money, baby girl."

"That's OK, you can make one out of paper and send it to me, that will be OK," I said.

"OK," he says.

"I love you, dad," I said

"I love you too, baby girl," he said.

I handed my mom the phone, excited to hear he was sending me a card. I was just as happy about the card as I was about him coming.

"I cannot wait to tell my friends my dad is sending me a card for my birthday!" I thought with excitement. "I'm going to tell their dads too that my dad is going to send me a beautiful birthday card."

As we walked home, it was getting dark. I wanted to walk faster so I could see my friends because I already knew they would be gone when the street lights came on.

By the time we finally reached the neighborhood, the street lights were on. I knew they weren't going to be outside.

"I'll tell them on the bus," I thought. "If I forget, I will send them a note in class," I thought, still excited about the card.

"Traci! Traci!" I said. "My dad is going to send

me a card for my birthday," I said in excitement.

Traci didn't seem excited about it and was not talking to me.

"I'm glad, so maybe you will leave my dad alone," she said.

My heart fell. I didn't understand why she said that and why she seemed so mad at me.

"Daddy is both of our dad's, Traci," I said.

"He's not your daddy!" my sister Traci shouted.

"Yes he is," I said angrily.

"No he is not! Your daddy's not here and my daddy is not your daddy!"

"Shut up! Yes he is!" I replied, holding back tears.

"No he is not, your daddy don't pay no child support, this is not even your house, this is mine and Mama's house."

"Shut up, Traci!"

"You shut up! You just want my daddy because your daddy don't want you."

"I hate you!" I said, running out of the room.

~◊~

"Mommy, did the mail come?" I asked as she walked in the front door.

"Not yet. What are you looking for, Staci?" Mommy asked.

"Dad said he is going to send me a card for my birthday this year," I said.

"Baby, your birthday was last month."

"I know, but maybe it's late because he is making it at home because he doesn't have the money to buy one," I said.

"Hmm," my mom said. "Why don't you go play with your friends?"

"I don't want to go outside. All they are going to do is pick at me," I said, crying and going to the bathroom.

I stood in the mirror and looked at myself. I had big brown eyes, shoulder-length hair and brown skin.

"Maybe I'm ugly," I thought. "Yes, that's it! He is ashamed of me because I'm ugly." I began to think. "I can get some makeup and make myself pretty so he would want me," I tell myself.

I continued to look in the mirror, trying to find any and everything wrong with me that could possibly be the reason he did not want me.

"What did I do? Why did he tell me another story?" I said, looking at myself and crying.

"Did I do something wrong for him to not want me? I will do better, I promise. God, please make my dad want me, I promise I will do better," I prayed.

I couldn't understand what was wrong. I thought about how Traci's dad always called, always came to see us, and he even did things with me. But I started to feel like Vanessa, Rachel and Traci were right, he was not my dad.

"I want my dad!" I thought.

My state of mind began to change from being upset to hatred and from hatred to rage. I did not want to be around anyone with a dad. I did not want to hear the word dad. He was no longer my dad. He was just a person I did not know. He was simply Timothy.

I tried to make myself not think about him. If my friends' dads came to school, to pick them up, to eat lunch with them or even if they got into trouble, I would secretly cry. If they asked me to their house, I would not go because I did not want to see them with their dad.

"I don't want to talk to nobody," I told myself.

Time passed and there still was no dad. I would make special food for my dad but no dad. I would run to the window when I heard a car but no dad. I still looked for mail from him but no mail. I decided to bury my thoughts about him, keep them secret from anybody, especially my new friends.

I started to do things little girls do without the thoughts of Timothy. It seemed to work very well. I would ignore any thoughts of him.

One day, a new friend came to my house. She had just moved in the neighborhood.

"Where is your dad?" she asked.

"I don't know where he is," I answered.

"Have you ever seen him?" she asked.

"I think so, but I don't remember," I replied.

"Hmmm," she said as I started to change the

subject. I could tell I wanted to cry and when she looked at me she could see my eyes turning red.

"It's OK, Staci, I don't know where my dad is either," she said.

"Really?" I said with excitement to know someone else was like me.

"Yup, but I don't care."

"Really?" I said. "How do you not care?" I asked.

"Oh, it's easy, just don't think about him," she said.

"Ohhhhh," I said. "I try that, but sometimes I still do."

"I did too, but after a while, I just stopped."

"Really?" I asked.

"Yup. Think about it this way. When we get grown, having a mother *and* a father in the house will be old school," she said, laughing.

"Ohhh," I said as I started laughing.

"It's OK. I am your friend and I won't leave you."

"OK," I said as she started to hug me.

I was so excited to have a friend like her. I didn't want to leave her side.

One day, mommy and I were walking to the store.

"You seem very happy, Staci. I'm glad to see you happy," she said.

"I have a new friend, Mommy, and she is amazing," I said.

"Well, that's good," she said as we walked into the store.

"You want something?" she asked.

"Yes," I said.

I got a cherry slushy and a slice of pound cake.

Mommy paid for the food and started talking to the cashier. I went outside to drink my slushy and eat my pound cake.

I looked at the pay phone on the wall outside of the store and smiled because I was not worried about calling Timothy anymore. As I stood against the window, a car pulled up. A little girl got out and her mother got out of the passenger side. Her dad got out of the driver's side and she ran to him and jumped in his arms.

"Daddy, can I get some candy and ice cream?" she asked.

"You can get whatever you want," he said.

"You are the best daddy in the whole wide world," she said.

As I watched, I became sad all over again. I stared as he hugged her and tickled her, walking inside the store. I no longer wanted to eat or drink. I did not want to be at the store. I started to cry, standing in my spot.

Mommy came out of the store and saw me crying.

"Staci, what's wrong?" she asked as I started to cry harder. "Staci, talk to me. You were just happy, what happened?"

I wouldn't say anything, I would only cry, dropping my slushy. Mommy looked around to see the man and his family in the store.

"Oh, Staci, I'm sorry, let's go," she said.

I continued to cry uncontrollably as she tried to hug me. I did not want her to hug me.

"Baby, please stop crying," she said. "Talk to

me."

"Mommy." I said between cries. "Where is my dad?"

"Right there," she said, and when I looked up, Daddy was pulling in the parking lot.

"Come on, Bonka," he said, calling me by the nickname he had given me.

At that moment, I knew that I had nothing to cry about, nothing to worry about, because he was there for me and loved me regardless of the fact that he wasn't my biological father. I was excited to see him and my tears quickly disappeared.

From the back Traci's head popped up.

"Come on, Staci, *our* daddy is here," she said, smiling.

From that moment on, I no longer asked, "Where is my dad?" because he was right there the entire time.

6 WHERE IS HOME?

"Yes, can I get a sausage biscuit and two cups of water?" my mother said, pushing her glasses closer to her face at the McDonald's drive through.

"That will be 87 cents," the cashier said.

"I don't have but 70 cents, Trish. Look in these seats and on the floor to see if we have any more change."

"OK," I said as I started to dig my hands between the seats. I did not want to move from my seat because of how cold it was inside of the car. I wrapped my coat tight and jumped in the back seat and pulled the seat out to find a nickel and three pennies.

I tried to look on the floor but it was dark outside so I could not see inside the car.

"Mama, can you turn on the light? I can't see the floor."

She turned the interior lights on and I started to look. I did not see any money on the floor.

126

"Hurry up, we are next," my mom said.

"I don't see anymore," I said as I climbed in the front seat. I began to dig in my seat again and opened the glove compartment, looking for any change.

"Stop looking. We are here now, I'm just going to give her the change and hope she doesn't count it," Mom said.

I handed her the eight cents that I found. The cashier handed her the water, then started counting the change.

"Ma'am, there's only 78 cents here," she said.

"Oh my goodness, I'm sorry, she must have miscounted," mama said, blaming the short amount on me. "Baby, hand me my pocketbook."

I looked around, confused because Mama doesn't carry a purse. As she looked in the car, I looked too, trying to find out if she had one hidden somewhere.

"Oh, goodness," she said. "I don't even have it with me."

"I'm sorry, ma'am, I cannot give you the sandwich," the cashier said.

"Oh, that's fine, I will be right back to get it. I cannot believe I do not have my pocketbook," she said. "Can we keep the water?"

"Yes, ma'am."

"OK. Thank you, we will be right back," Mama said.

"OK," the cashier said.

"We are going to have to go to another McDonald's to see if we can get something to eat. OK, Trish?" Mama said, driving away.

"OK." I said.

My stomach was starting to growl loudly from not eating in two days. I laid my head against the window and thought about different foods I wanted to eat.

"Mama, remember when we made hotdogs and noodles on the Kerosene heater?"

"Yeah, I wish we had that right now," she said. "We are pulling up now, the lobby should be open. Just run inside and use the bathroom and I'll wait and go in after you come out," Mama said. "I'm sure you have to go."

"OK," I said.

We pulled up at another McDonalds and I got out and went in. I walked in the bathroom and closed the door. My face in the mirror did not look like the face of a 14 year old. I looked old, dirty, and tired.

I walked into the stall to use the bathroom. As I was using it, I tried to take one of the toilet rolls off, but it would not come off so I rolled as much as I could off and stuffed it in all of my pants and jacket pockets. I wasn't quite ready to button my pants so I left them unbuttoned and partly down.

I flushed the toilet with a piece of tissue and opened the door with the same tissue and threw it in the trash can that was attached to the wall.

I turned the water on, waiting for it to get warm but it never got warm. I splashed the water on my face and walked over to the paper towel with my face dripping water to dry my face.

I grabbed more paper towels, put the soap from the dispenser on it, wet it and started to wipe my vagina to ensure that it was clean. I threw those paper towels away and grabbed more, put some more soap on it and wiped under my arms.

I took a deep breath as I looked at myself in the mirror. I tried to lift my eyes and cheeks with my hands but they fell right back down when I let go. I started to button up my shorts and grabbed another paper towel to open the door so I could leave. I walked as quickly as I could, with my head down, out of the restaurant.

As I approached the car, I did not see Mama. I began to panic as daylight was approaching.

"Where is she?" I said out loud, as if someone would have answered.

I looked in the windows of our old rusted 1966 Duster and did not see the keys in the ignition. I pulled on the cold handle and it did not open.

"She would never leave the door unlocked," I thought as I kept pulling.

"Trish!" I heard and immediately turned around. "Let's go," Mama said.

Mama was walking fast with a bag and cup in her hand.

"OK," I said, confused.

She got to the car and because of my hunger, I immediately smelled the food in the bag. She unlocked her door, placed the bag and drink inside and leaned over to unlock my door. I jumped in the car as fast as I could.

"Mama, how did you get food?" I asked.

"I had to lie, baby, I told them that they messed up my order yesterday," Mama said, starting the car.

"But we weren't here yesterday, Mama." I said.

"I know, God will have to forgive me later," she said. "Open the bag, Trish, get a sandwich and hash brown and eat. Drink some of that coffee so you can get warm."

I opened the bag and could not even get the paper off of the sandwich fast enough to start eating. I handed her the other sandwich and hash brown and she ate as fast as she could. I sipped on the coffee but could not drink it because I did not like the taste.

"Where are we going?" I asked.

"Well, it's Monday and you have to go to school to make sure that you eat your breakfast and lunch."

'I have a test Mama. I haven't studied," I said.

"You have to go so you can eat," she said.

"OK," I said, dropping my head. "I'll save some for you too, Mama. I'll put some in my book bag."

"I'll be just fine. Make sure you eat," she said.

I sat in my seat, so full I wanted to fall asleep. We pulled into a nearby park as the sun started to peek out.

"Come on," she said, taking the keys from the ignition.

I opened my door and walked to the trunk as she was sticking the key in to open it.

"How long…" I started, but she quickly interrupted me.

"Don't ask," she said. "I don't know, baby, I just don't know."

Mama opened the trunk and I stared at it as it looked like a huge pile of junk. Clothes, shoes, pillows, blankets. Our whole house was in the trunk…well, what we could stuff in the trunk was.

Mama grabbed a shirt, pants and underwear. The shoes she grabbed had more holes in it than the ones I had on so I told her I would just wear the ones I had.

I took the clothes and got back in the car to change my clothes. She closed the trunk and got back in the car so she could take me to school.

We got to school and the parking lot waiting for the school to open. I dozed off and it seemed like just two minutes before Mama started shaking my leg, telling me it was time to get up.

I woke up and grabbed my book bag.

"I'll be right back so I can give you some food," I said.

"I'm OK. The sandwich and hash brown was just enough," she said.

I walked to school and straight to the cafeteria. I grabbed my plate and stood in line. When my time came up, I looked at the food and asked for a donut and fruit. When I got to the end of the line I picked up two chocolate milks.

"56 cents," the lunch lady said.

"Huh?" I said.

"It's 56 cents for your breakfast."

"But my mama paid for my lunch this month," I said.

"There is no payment. You can't get that unless you have the 56 cents," she said.

"What if I put the other chocolate milk back?" I asked.

"Then it will be 50 cents," she said taking, the extra milk off my tray.

"I don't have 50 cents," I said.

"Then go back and get a peanut butter sandwich. You can't have this," she said, taking my tray from me.

I walked back to get the sandwich as the other kids started to laugh at me.

"You can get water from the water fountain," she said.

"Yes, ma'am," I said, walking to a table.

I opened my book bag and tore two sheets of paper out of my notebook. I used the paper to wrap around the sandwich and put it in my book bag.

"She stealing the food," I heard someone say.

I did not say anything, I took my book bag and left the cafeteria. I walked straight to the bathroom. I walked in the stall, closed the door, sat on the toilet and cried. I was so embarrassed at having to leave my food. I didn't understand why Mama hadn't paid for the lunch for the month and on top of that, why she didn't tell me? I heard people coming in the bathroom and I got off the toilet and used tissue to flush it as if I had used the bathroom.

I walked out of the bathroom to see three girls looking at me. One of the girls laughed at me because she saw the lunch lady take my plate. I walked to the sink, washed and dried my hands, and as I was walking out of the door I heard one of the girls talking.

"She always looks so dirty," she said as they all laughed.

I walked down the hall to my class. When I walked in the door, my teacher was standing at the metal pencil sharpener sharpening pencils for the test. I went near the back of the room and sat in a desk.

"Good morning, Trish, you're mighty early this morning," my teacher said as she was sharpening pencils for the test. "You are normally late or not here."

"Good morning, ma'am," I said.

I laid my head down on the desk to try and get a little sleep before everyone started to come in class.

"Mrs. Stone!" I heard another teacher say.

"Mrs. Stone!"

"Yes," Mrs. Stone said.

"Can you help me with this?" she said as I started to hear a lot of commotion.

Mrs. Stone got up from her desk and students started piling in the doorway with what seemed like a fight that had broken out.

"Get inside that classroom and have a seat," Mrs. Stone told the students.

Most of the students were not even in my class, but she wanted them out of harm's way.

"There goes my sleep," I thought to myself as students started to pile in.

Nobody wanted to sit near me. They all sat at desks that were not close to me or moved their desks away from me.

I didn't respond in any way. I was just sleepy so I wanted to go to sleep. The students talked amongst themselves, laughing and joking about the weekend they had with friends. This made me depressed because my weekend was spent riding around in the car and visiting people to be able to go inside a house.

Students from outside class started to come in the class and Mrs. Stone called the students out that were not a part of our class as the tardy bell rang. Mrs. Stone started calling role and as soon as I heard my name, I began to doze off.

I was trying to stay awake but my eyes were so heavy. My head was bobbing back and forth from trying to keep it straight, yet the sleep was pulling it down. Mrs. Stone began to pass out the test, giving the first person in the row enough for everyone in the row. We passed the test around and waited for her to tell us when to start.

Once she told us when to start, she walked to the chalkboard and wrote the end time.

"You have until 11:45 to finish the test," she said.

I looked at the test and it seemed as if the letters and words were jumping all over the page.

What seemed like a 30 second nod ended up being my entire class period. I was awakened by the sounds of classmates leaving and entering the classroom. I reached down to grab my book bag and saw a baby roach climbing out of it.

"Oh no!" I said, looking around to see if anyone saw it. I kicked the bag to knock it off and picked up my book bag.

"Trish," I heard as I was walking to the door.

"Yes, ma'am," I said.

"Are you ok? You are the smartest student in my class, but it seems you are not able to concentrate," Mrs. Stone said.

"Yes, ma'am, I'm OK," I said.

"Sweetheart, if you could get here every day and on time, you would be amazed at how well you can do. You are almost an honor student now and you are barely here. Do you know your potential?" she asked.

"No, ma'am," I said.

"You don't?"

"No, ma'am," I said.

"Sweetheart…" she started before the tardy bell rang for the next class.

"Look, I'll give you a late note, take it. Go on to class and be sure we talk tomorrow, OK?"

"Yes, ma'am," I said.

The day had passed and it was time for me to

leave. As everyone was rushing out of the door, I was careful to not let anyone bump me because of the breakfast and lunch food I had in my book bag. I stood back in the hall, watching everyone go out the door, looking at my mom sitting in the old beat up car waiting for me. I was so embarrassed by the car, I would wait until everyone left before I would go to it.

I got in the car and asked where we were going.

"We are going to Joann's house for a few hours," she said.

"Oh, so we are not going to stay the night?" I asked.

"No."

"It's already cold in the car and it's going to be colder tonight and the covers don't work and the heat don't…"

"You will just get in one spot and not move. That spot will stay warm," she said. "I don't have no money for a thermostat, we need gas and food. I'm driving around here and need glasses, I can't see out of these glasses because they are so old. I'm still trying to find people to borrow money from so we can get gas in the car," she said.

"OK." I said, looking out the window with

tears forming in my eyes.

"We will be at her house long enough to warm up and then leave."

"OK," I said, still looking out the window. "Are we going to eat there too?"

"I don't know," she said.

"I have some breakfast and some of the pizza from lunch in my book bag so we can share it later, OK?" I said.

Mama didn't reply. She just kept driving as I watched the passing trees, homes, and cars out of the window. Every time I saw a house or trailer, it was almost like I wanted to be able to see through the brick or siding into the house. I would wonder if it were warm inside, if they had food, or if they were happy. I wished so badly that we had a home to go to.

I noticed we were close to one of my friend's houses and I began to think that I did not want to go to her friend Joann's house.

"Can I go see my friend Teresa?" I asked.

"OK, but you can't stay long," she said.

As she started in the direction of Teresa house,

I began to think of ways I would try to prolong the visit so we could stay later at Joann's house, if we still went there. Although I didn't want to go, at least it would be warm that night.

We arrived at the gate to Teresa's house and I noticed large lights.

"Oh, no," I thought, because I knew what was going to happen because of the lights.

Teresa stayed on a military installation and Mama wasn't military, so they pulled us over to inspect the car. My heart dropped. Sometimes they would just wave us in or she used a form from one of her old boyfriends, but this time they stopped us.

"Mama, it's OK, let's just go to Ms. Joann's house," I said.

"It's too late now, what's the matter?" she asked.

I began to scoot as far down in the car as I could. I did not want the soldiers to see me in the car.

"License and registration, please?" one of the military police asked my mom.

"OK," she said.

"Open that glove compartment and get my registration," she told me as she opened the ash tray and took her license out.

I did not want to move, I was already somewhat warm in my coat. I opened the glove compartment and gave her the registration and tried to hide my face.

Another military police officer walked to my side of the car and asked me to get out of the car. I wrapped the coat around me tight and got out of the car. As I was getting out, I heard the other officer tell Mama to get out of the car.

They started using mirrors to look under the car, and asked Mama to open the trunk, hood and glove compartment so they could check inside. They checked the inside of the car and closed the doors. The officer took Mama to the front of the car so she could witness him checking under the hood. One of the officers asked me to stand at the back of the car with him while she and the officer checked under the hood. I was dreading them looking in the trunk.

She walked to the back of the car without a care in the world and opened the trunk.

"Wow," I heard the officer beside me say with the exposure of everything that was in the trunk.

It looked as if Mama had added even more things in the trunk. The officer beside me walked to the back of the trunk and I stood back, not wanting to go near the car.

"Come here, Trish," Mama said, wanting me to hold some of the items from the trunk so that they could try and search deeper in the trunk.

I dropped my head, embarrassed, and walked to the trunk. As I reached the trunk, I could see a license plate that wasn't in there before, more clothes, a dish drain, cups and more. My pillow and cover were underneath all of the things that was added.

I stood, embarrassed, as they used batons to push and move around everything in the trunk. I just wanted them to hurry up so I could get in the car.

"Thank you, ma'am," one of the officers said, handing Mama her driver's license and registration.

I rushed to my side of the car, hopped in and held my coat tight. Mama got in the car as though nothing remotely bothered her about what had just taken place. We arrived at my friend's house and I was excited to be able to go inside and sit down. Her house was always so beautiful and clean, I just wanted to enjoy it for as long as I could.

I rang the doorbell and waited. Her mother opened the door, greeting me with a big smile.

"Hi, baby!" she said with excitement.

"Hi, Ms. Jones," I said.

"Teresa isn't here, baby, she is gone to the store in town," she said.

"Oh, OK," I said as positively as I could, knowing I was crushed at not being able to go inside.

"I'll tell her you came by," she said. "She has been trying to call you for about a week now, but the phone isn't working."

"Oh no, ours is not on yet because we moved," I said.

"Oh, OK. Well, when they turn the new one on, make sure you give us your new number," she said.

"Yes, ma'am. Bye-bye," I said.

"Bye, baby."

My heart was crushed at the fact that I could not see Teresa and we might not be at Ms. Joann's house late enough to stay the night.

We arrived at Ms. Joann's house as dusk-dark

was approaching. I wrapped my coat tightly around me and started walking to the door when Mama stopped me.

"Trish," she said. "Come get the blankets and pillows so we can put them in the back seat."

"OK," I said, walking back to the car.

Mama was moving around everything in the trunk in get to the pillows and blankets. I grabbed a pillow and the blankets and she grabbed another pillow.

"I want to go ahead and take these out so we don't have to get out when we leave," she said.

"OK," I said.

We walked to the door and when Ms. Joann answered the door, a bask of warm air flowed out, which felt like heaven to me. I was so glad to feel warmth that I walked in, even before Ms. Joann asked us in.

"I'm sorry," I said.

"Oh, it's OK. Everybody is in the back."

I was taken aback by the wonderful smell of freshly fried pork chops, chicken, vegetables and I could even smell the starch from the boiling rice.

On the table was homemade macaroni and cheese and a golden brown pound cake. My stomach began to growl loudly and my mouth began to water as I looked at the table. I felt a nudge and when I looked behind me, it was Mama giving me the look of death.

I walked to the back to see all of the young teenagers talking, watching television, and enjoying themselves. I wanted to just lay down in the nice queen size bed that was full of kids playing Atari.

"Hi, Trish!" several of them said.

"Hey," I said, looking around in the room. Ms. Joann's kids James, Kim, Nick and Rob were there, but I did not recognize the others in the room.

"Take your coat off and throw it on the floor, let's play," James said.

"Oh, I'm OK," I said, not wanting to take my coat off because I had not showered in over a week and I was still cold from the car.

I remembered Ms. Joann always kept extra clean washcloths in her bathroom.

"I'll be right back," I said, getting up to go to the bathroom that was connected to the bedroom.

I closed the door and immediately turned on the

sink. I did not want to turn on their shower because I didn't want them to hear me taking a shower in their house and I did not want to be teased. I took off my clothes, my socks, which were semi wet and hard in spots, and my shoes. I grabbed one of the washcloths, lathered it up, and washed my entire body with the washcloth. I washed everything from the back of my ears to the soles of my feet.

Each time I wrung the washcloth out, I could see the brown residue from the washcloth because the only washing I had done was in sinks of gas stations that would allow us to use the bathrooms and fast food restaurants. There were no washcloths in them, and sometimes no paper towels, only tissue.

I put back on my clothes, my socks, shoes, and my coat. I took the washcloth and put it in my coat pocket so I could use it at the restaurants or gas stations. I flushed the toilet, waited a few minutes, and then turned the sink off.

When I walked back in the room, no one was in there. There were controllers, papers, pillows and clothes all over the bed but no one there. I could hear laughter and talking coming from the kitchen, so I started to walk out the door and noticed Mama sitting on the floor sleep.

"Mama," I said as Nick walked and one of his

friends walked in the room.

Mama looked up, with her glasses barely on her face and Nick said "Bright light," as he turned on the light switch.

"Mama is looking for you," Nick said.

"OK. I'm coming," she said.

"We are in the kitchen," he said, walking out.

We went into the kitchen to see that everyone was sitting down eating. My eyes lit up because the food looked so good.

"Come on, Trish, let's go," Mama said.

"Huh?" I said.

"Y'all leaving?" Ms. Joann said.

"Oh, yes, we have to go," Mama said.

"Oh, OK, girl, I will see you later," Ms. Joann said.

I became furious. I could not understand and with all the food in my face, I wanted to eat too. Mama pushed me out of the door and I began to cry, storming to the car.

When she opened the door, all I could smell

was the chicken scent from our clothes.

"Mama, why didn't we eat?" I asked.

"Trish, couldn't you tell that was a gathering she was having for her kids and their friends? It is rude to sit around eating at other people tables," she said.

"But…" I started.

"Shut up! Just shut up!" she said driving off.

It was blistering cold, in the lower teens that night. We drove and I was still very upset about not eating.

"We are about to run out of gas," Mama said, pulling into the hospital parking lot.

"Let's go," she said.

"Someone sick?" I asked.

"No, we are going to sit in the lobby of the emergency room like we are waiting on someone so we can stay warm," she said.

I grabbed my book bag and gave her half of the breakfast and lunch, which was nearly frozen, that I took from school.

"When we go in here, make sure you get some

water to wash this down," she said.

We went inside the hospital emergency room waiting room and found a corner. I sat beside the window where I could see the cars in the parking lot coming and leaving. I watched people coming in and leaving the parking lot and would imagine where they were going and what their houses looked like.

I turned to Mama as she started dozing off.

"Mama, how long are we going to live in the car?" I asked.

"I don't know," she mumbled, half asleep.

I sat, thinking about my test in school the next day, wondering how long we would be on the streets and wishing I had a different life altogether. I thought about my teacher when she said I had potential and became sad because if she was right, I did not have what I needed to reach the potential.

I looked at Mama as she slept and wanted to walk away and leave her there and find someone who would be able to give me a place to stay, but I began to feel like I couldn't just leave her there.

I pulled my coat as tight as I could even though it was getting much warmer and decided to fall asleep.

"Whoever is out there," I prayed to myself. "Could you do something for me? Could you please…please, show me where home is?" I said and fell asleep to the rumbling of my stomach.

7 THAT HURTS

I watched out the window, hating to see the sun go down. Fear started to set in as I watched the sky turn dusk-dark. I opened my eyes as big as I could to look for the sun, but it was gone.

"It's night time again. I have to close my door before he comes in here. I am afraid he may hear me close my door. I will do it real slow so that he does not know that I am closing the door. I know he is up there drinking and will be in here real soon. My mom went to work already so I know he is just giving her enough time to be gone before he comes in here. I will put on some shorts, long pants, and two shirts and wrap up real tight in my covers. Maybe he will forget tonight. Maybe he will pass out sleep," I thought to myself, running around my room trying to figure a way to protect myself. "Maybe if I stay completely still, he won't bother me. I have to breath very soft. I can't make any sound at all," I told myself.

I rounded up my clothes. I wouldn't even take a shower because I didn't want to wake him up with the noise if he was asleep. I put on my layers of clothes and headed to my closet. I slowly, very slowly closed my door so that no sound was made. I rushed to my closet to get all the shoes I could find and put them against the door.

"Maybe he cannot open the door. I will make a line from the door to the wall so they will push against each other and he can't get in," I said to myself.

I jumped in the bed and wrapped the covers and sheets around me real tight. I looked around the room and rapid thoughts began to walk in my mind.

"Why does she let him stay here when she is at work?" I began to think.

I tried to keep as quiet as possible.

"I don't like him. I am so tired," I thought to myself. I never got to sleep at night because my sleep was always interrupted and I always ended up hurting so I could never go back to sleep. Sometimes I wanted to go to sleep on the bus on my way to school or in class but it was always so loud, I couldn't sleep there, either.

"Ahh," I thought to myself as it seemed the coast was finally clear. I just might be able to sleep, and I was happy that maybe it worked.

"Come here." I was awakened by him standing over me, pulling the covers off. I was terrified. I was so scared. He was stronger than me so he always got the covers off. He took all of my clothes off and looked at me. He proceeded to do what he did every night and I had to just lay there and not say anything.

"I wonder how he got in the room. Why didn't the shoes stop him? Why didn't I hear him come in?" I thought.

I looked around to see he had the door closed. I didn't want the door closed with him in here. Somebody please help me. Something about this didn't feel right.

He was so heavy and I could not move. He was always hurting me 'down there', every night when my mom went to work. All I could think about is how long would it be tonight? How long after this would I be hurting? What was it exactly that he was doing to me that caused me to hurt so much? Why did he like to do this to me when it hurt me so bad? Was this normal? All I could smell was his body and alcohol. I couldn't breathe.

Tonight was different. I saw something that I hadn't seen before.

"What is that white stuff?" I asked him.

"Nothing, don't worry about it," he says, leaving the room.

I no longer cried about the pain. I just lay there afterwards. I sometimes felt stuff like water coming out of my privates but I didn't feel that tonight.

He walked back in the room with a washcloth and used it to wipe the white stuff off of my privates and my stomach. I put my clothes back on and covered myself up real tight because I knew he was going to lay in my bed.

I laid there, thinking how every time we went to his house, I never wanted to get out of the car. He called me to his room over and over. I always wanted to stay with my mom but he kept calling. My mom always walked around the house talking to family as he closes me in the room with him. He opened my legs and hurt me while my mom was in the house.

My thoughts were interrupted because like clockwork, here he comes to lay in the bed. He took all my clothes back off and lay in the bed, pulling me up against him. I hated him. He was so gross. He was a monster. He was the real boogieman.

~◊~Story 2~◊~

"No, no, no!" I said, smelling loud cologne. "Stop!" I screamed as I saw his sinister smile leaning in to kiss me on the cheek. I could feel his rough hair on my face.

"Please, just leave me alone," I said to him, but it fell on deaf ears.

I told myself that this time I was going to fight. I was going to be a big girl because I did not like what he did to me. I was going to fight and kick and punch and bite. My mom might be mad because I did it, but I was scared of him.

As he leaned in I started to scream, fight, punch and bite him.

"Am I hitting him?" I said as my tiny arms seemed to strike dead air. "Can anyone hear me?" I think as I screamed louder and louder.

As I am punching as hard as I can, he grabbed me by the shoulders and started shaking me.

"Token!" he said, calling me by my nickname. "Token!" he said again.

I did not answer him. I only screamed and kicked and fought him.

"Token! Token! Token!" I continued to hear as I was being shaken.

A light slap hit my face and I woke up.

"Are you OK?" my friend Johnathan asked.

"Yes," I said, looking around to see where I was.

"You were fighting in your sleep, Token," Johnathan said.

"I was?" I asked.

"Yes and screaming STOP!" one of my littlest friends said. He was only 6. He and others mimicked what I was doing in my sleep.

"Did you have a dream about the boogieman?" he asked.

"Yes," I said softly, a bit embarrassed about me fighting in my sleep.

"Your mom is on her way," Johnathan's mom said.

"I know," I said, letting out sigh, dreading to go with her because I already knew where we were going.

"Bonk! Bonk!" I heard and knew it was my mom's car horn.

I said bye to all my friends as I left, already knowing what I was going to.

We rode for a little while until we got to a house that was very familiar to me. I was safe in this house because I knew he wasn't there. We went inside and I was very comfortable laughing and playing with the grown-ups and some of the little kids like me there.

A knock came on the door.

"Come in," I heard from one of the grown-ups.

I ran and peeked around the corner and my heart dropped.

"Oh my God!" I said out loud, rushing to cover my mouth so he couldn't hear me.

"Here he comes," I thought to myself as I saw him heading in my direction. "Please, Mom, don't go near him," I thought as he was talking to her.

"Why does he always have to come around? I don't like him," I thought to myself, becoming angry. "Why do you always want to kiss me? Don't

you know that your scraggly beard and loud
cologne always makes me scared when I see or
smell it on other grown men that I see? You are
always nice to me around my mom and family and
you are not ever mean to me but you always touch
my privates when they are not around. That hurts!"
I said to myself, full of anger and rage.

I continued to stare at him, feeling as though I
could cut him with my eyes. My hands, no bigger
than half his hands, I could see slapping him for
trying to kiss my cheek. As he talked to my mother,
I continued talking to myself, expressing all the
anger that I was afraid to express to him.

"I hate to see you coming because I know you
want to give me a kiss. I know you want to take me
to the store. The last time you took me, you pulled
me over to you and opened my legs and stuck your
fingers in my privates as we drove down the street.
That really hurt! I tried to get the man in the truck
beside us to help me and even mouthed to him to
help me because he could see where your hands
were. He laughed at me and drove off. I wanted to
cry but I did not want you to know how bad you
hurt me. I wanted you to see that I am a strong little
girl. I guess it's better because at least you don't
hurt me every night the way that the other one does
but you still hurt my privates when you always do
that!" I thought with anger.

"Token! Token!" I heard you call. "Do you want to go to the store?"

I did not answer. I was trying to get past you without being seen so I could lock myself in the bathroom.

"Token?" my mom called as they started walking towards me. I ran and hid by the tall house plant as they walked past me and then I ran to the bathroom.

"She just ran in there," one of the kids said.

"In where?" my mom asked as I could hear her starting to walk towards the bathroom.

"Token, let's go to the store," he said.

I started to cringe, then I started to cry.

"What are you doing in there?" my mom asked, knocking on the door.

"I'm using the bathroom."

"OK, hurry up, he is going to take you to the store to buy you some candy. Don't you want to go?"

"I'm going to be in here a long time," I said, dragging the long out.

"It's OK, I will wait for you," he said.

I sat down on the toilet with all my clothes on trying to take a long time so he would leave. I began to sit and talk to myself as if I were talking to him.

"Why do you do that? Is that what little girls are supposed to do, let you do that? I worry about your daughters because do you do that to them too? Do you do that to their mom? When she hugs me, why don't she touch my privates like you do? Do you tell her?" I said, not knowing I was talking too loud.

"Who are you talking too?" my mom asked.

"Myself," I said.

"Come on, baby girl, so I can take you to the store," he said.

I started to cry, but then I realized I had to be a big girl. I wiped my face and opened the door. As soon as I opened it, he was standing there with his beard, Afro, and shirt half unbuttoned, with a necklace and chest hairs sticking out. The strong cologne hit me in the face as soon as I opened the door.

"Are you ready baby girl?" he said, and I stared at him, talking to him with my mind.

"Can I ask you if is that normal? I'm so confused because my mom doesn't believe me when I tell her about you and the boogie man but you both keep doing it and I don't like it. You are just like the boogieman, you are a bad man, a scary man."

He reached his hand out for my hand and I looked at my mom as if I wanted her to rescue me.

"We will be right back," he said.

I began to act like a big girl because I already knew what was going to happen in the car. I began to tell myself that I was saving his daughters because they are so much smaller than me. I decided to just let him hurt my cootie-cat instead of them because they were so little.

That made me a big girl....Right?

BONUS

SUNDAY MORNING

An old folk short story

As I lay here in bed covered with homemade-quilted comforters, wool socks and mittens on my hands to keep warm, I peek through to see if it is daylight outside. I can tell it is near morning by the smell of kerosene, the wood in the iron fireplace burning, and gas from the oven, which Mama has turned on to begin breakfast.

I lay here afraid to move from my spot 'cause I know that once I get up, the house will be cold. You see, we ain't got the best heating and the snow is up to the doorsteps.

Old man winter came early this year. Papa said he didn't make enough money at the mill to buy mo' plastic fo' the windows so we had to use flimsy clothes and trash bags to try to keep the cold out.

I can hear the wind outside hitting the old and worn wind chimes Uncle Tommy made. The wind sounds eager to come in the house.

I can hear the pots and pans clanging against one another as Mama begins to cook. I can hear her swishing water around in the sink so I can only imagine it's to keep her hands clean while she is cooking.

I can hear her singing a tune rather loudly,

"Jesus, Jesus, oh how I love calling your name."

I can imagine her bopping around the kitchen as she sings Shirley Caesar's song. She often will hum or sing to express her feelings of how she loves God.

The soft, beautiful gospel hymns and the soft pitter patter of her feet across the old wooden floor helps to put me back to sleep.

I am awakened by the sweet smell of honey bacon. Mama loves to put it in the oven and let the smell flow through the house like a breeze of warmth on a cool day. I hear the sausage sizzling on the stove and smell those homemade biscuits as they begin to rise. I hear her beating the oranges on the counter to make the oranges just soft enough that when she cuts it, it will pour the juice into the large jar smoothly with a gentle squeeze.

"OH MY LORD!" I hear her abruptly say which means she must have cut herself on a piece of fatback.

I lay here and smile as I can envision Mama in her house coat with those old, dirty, torn house shoes along with that old torn apron that has patches and holes everywhere. Mama used one of the patches that I made at school last year for my 2nd grade project grade.

I can see her using her forearms to wipe away the sweat from standing over the stove. She has managed to put flour in her hair and on her face but she still has a smile as she walks to the table. She is setting the table with Papa at the head, of course, and me and little Nate beside each other on one side.

On the other side she sets the table for a little abused boy she has taken from his parents, and my cousin whose mom died 2 years ago.

I hear the roosters beginning to crow. You see, Mama has a yard full of chickens, pigs and, well, she had a garden, but the snow took all of that. But it will be back in plenty of time for me to help her in the summer again.

I hear the door open and slam shut. The spring on the door is old and rusted and it don't work very well. It just slams that wood against the frame. Papa keeps on saying he is going to fix that door but Uncle Tommy says he is going to teach little Nate how to do it and we are still waiting for little Nate to learn.

I know that mama is going to get the eggs from the chickens, though, because I can hear her humming outside by the coup.

I can tell I need to go ahead and get ready for breakfast now. My mouth is watering from the smells in the air. I sit up in the bed and my feet hit the hard, wooden floor. I look around the room and it seems kinda gloomy. As I head down the hallway the dogs begin to bark.

The only time they bark is when Uncle Tommy is swaying down the dirt road towards the house. You see, he goes out and gets drunk every Saturday night and tries to come over on Sunday mornings for breakfast. Mama, being as nice as she is, just sets another place at the table for him and tells him, "Boy! You better wash yo self 'fore you set at my table, you been out there doing God knows what and you ain't gonna bring it here. Now go on, boy, get cleaned up"!

As I look at myself in the mirror, it seems so foggy. It almost seems dreamlike. With the sleep still in my eyes I can smell the soft smell of cinnamon and nutmeg.

"Sweet potato pie!" I say out loud. "Mama is going to make a sweet potato pie for dinner."

Now I know I can't wait to get out of church so I can come home for some of her sweet potato pie.

I hurry up and wash my face with only the cold water that she has in a bucket with a towel she has laid out. I have to use the bathroom but I don't want my warm behind exposed to use the house bucket so I try to wait. I run back to my room and find the prettiest little dress I can find and some tights.

My shoes are old with a hole in the toe but they will be OK for church. Mama says that God don't care what you dress in as long as you pay attention.

Strangely, I hear the screen door slam shut again but then I think it's probably Uncle Tommy who has finally made his way in or Mama who came back in the house. I begin to walk on towards the kitchen.

Our hallway is long with some holes in the walls and pictures. There is a picture of my great-grandma who was a slave before. She was so beautiful. She looks just like my mama. Another picture was my mama and my great-grandma with this little hair bow that my great-grandma gave my mama and my mama gave me. I lost it though and I am too afraid to tell Mama.

I see the soft flicker of the kerosene heater in the middle of the hallway. It looks as though it's about to go out. I stare at a calendar on the wall. Today is Sunday, November 22nd and although this is another Sunday morning this morning seems very familiar.

My eyebrows squint a little as though there is something I should remember about today. I pull my house coat as tightly as I can with my wool socks and my slippers on awaiting to turn the corner and grab Mama and say good morning Mama. The smells and flavors of the foods are so strong yet so distant.

As I turn the corner something strange has happened. There is no food, no smells, no table set, no Uncle Tommy, no little Nate. I can't understand what is happening. I look outside and there is no snow. The old dirt road isn't dirt anymore and there is a gas station directly in sight. The old rugged stop sign is not in sight.

I run to the back and there is no garden, no chickens, and no shed full of Papa's stuff. I stand there, puzzled and unresponsive. I go to the door that I am positive I heard open and shut. When I look down, I notice a small piece of hair jewelry. It is the bow that I had lost.

"Where did this come from?" I say.

I go back down the hallway and am stop by the calendar. November 22nd is all too familiar now. Mama died 22 years ago this Sunday morning. I think I get it now. Mama just wanted to say hello.

ABOUT THE AUTHOR

L. Trott-Spivey is a Bermudian-American raised by her Guyanese Father and American Mother. She was born in Brooklyn, New York. She is the mother of three beautiful children. She received her undergrad at both Central Texas College and Columbia College of Fort Stewart, Georgia. She also obtained Master's in Human Resources Management from Webster University, Fort Stewart, Georgia. She is currently a State of Georgia Employee, business owner, and writer.

She has seen her fair share of trials and tribulations which has inspired her to begin writing. She has found that writing is her peace of mind and a great joy for her on a rainy day. She also enjoys singing, dancing, and meditating, and spending quality time with her family.